Pet
Finders
Club

Dachshund in Danger!

by Ben M. Baglio

Cover art by Andrew Beckett
Interior art by Meg Aubrey

SCHOLASTIC INC.

New York   Toronto   London   Auckland   Sydney
Mexico City   New Delhi   Hong Kong   Buenos Aires

ISBN 0-439-79251-7

12 11 10 9 8 7 6 5 4 3 2 1   6 7 8 9 10 11/0

Printed in the U.S.A.
First Scholastic printing, March 2006

Special thanks to Liss Norton

Chapter One

Andi Talbot turned up her collar against the January sleet and tried to smile at her friend Natalie Lewis. "I love taking Bud out, but it won't be tough going back inside today. It's freezing!"

Natalie tucked the ends of her purple scarf into her padded jacket. "Totally!" she agreed, shivering.

Andi's cute tan-and-white Jack Russell terrier raced up when he heard his name. He jumped up, his mouth open in a wide doggy grin, then charged away across the park. Natalie's black Labrador, Jet, galloped after him, his ears streaming backward.

"Don't look now," Andi warned, pointing to a deep patch of mud, too wide for Jet to jump.

"Jet, no!" Natalie yelled.

To Andi's relief, Buddy dodged the puddle and sat down on the other side with his tongue hanging out.

Unfortunately, Jet didn't follow. He bounded straight into the mud, splashing it all over his shiny black coat.

"Oh, no," Natalie moaned. "Come here, Jet! And sit!"

Jet sat down in the puddle.

"I didn't mean sit *there*. I meant come *out* and sit down!" Natalie sighed, then began to giggle.

Andi started laughing, too. "Good thing we're on the way to obedience class," she said. "Now that Jet has learned *sit*, maybe he can learn *come*."

Natalie rolled her eyes. "I wish." She patted her knees. "Come on, Jet! Get out of there."

Jet trotted to her and wagged his tail against her jeans, smearing them with mud. "You're totally impossible," Natalie said. She ruffled his ears and gave him a dog treat. "What is Fisher going to say when he sees you?"

"He won't mind," Andi said. Fisher Pearce, the local ASPCA veterinarian, ran the dog-training classes. "He's crazy about dogs." She glanced at Jet and grinned. "Even muddy ones."

The dog-training classes were held in a spacious room behind the ASPCA center. Through the brightly lit windows, Andi and Natalie could see people inside, moving around with their dogs. Andi felt a twinge of excitement. This was her first visit to Natalie's class, and she couldn't wait to meet all the dogs and their owners.

"There's Gemma," Natalie said, pointing to a dark-haired girl aged about fourteen. A gorgeous chestnut-and-white Cocker spaniel was bouncing around her ankles. "And that's Crumble," Natalie added. "You'll love him."

They pushed the door open and went into a narrow entrance hall. "I'll get some paper towels so we can try to clean Jet up," Andi said. She got some from the bathroom, and she and Natalie started rubbing his thick black fur. Jet licked Natalie's face. "He thinks you're dirty, too," Andi joked.

A broad-shouldered man wearing faded denim overalls arrived, leading a very lively black-and-white-spotted crossbreed puppy. Andi guessed it had some Dalmatian in its ancestry.

"Evening, Natalie," the man said.

"Hi, Mr. Taylor! How's Dapple doing?"

"Not too bad. He's down to chewing through only two pairs of sneakers a day now. It looks like Jet had a fun walk!" He grinned. "Hi there," he said to Andi. "Are you starting classes today?"

"No, Buddy and I are just watching," Andi replied. She

took a break from helping Natalie to give Dapple a pat. The adorable puppy twisted his head to lick her hand.

"This is my friend, Andi," Natalie said.

"Well, I hope you enjoy the class, Andi." Mr. Taylor stroked Buddy's head before going through the swinging doors that led into the main room.

The door opened again and a tan-and-black German shepherd bounded in, tugging a tiny woman behind him. "Wait, Prince!" she called. "Oh, hi, Natalie." The woman yanked on Prince's leash, but he dragged her straight past them without stopping.

"Hey, Jan!" Natalie called after her. She shook her head. "Prince hasn't gotten the hang of heeling yet." She straightened up, wiping her hands on her muddy jeans. "Come on, Jet. You're as clean as we're going to get you."

Andi and Natalie threw away the muddy paper towels and went into the classroom. Fisher Pearce was on the other side of the room, bending down to a plump and hairy Pekingese. "See you later, Chester." He ruffled the little dog's fur and headed to greet Natalie and Andi. "Hi, you two. Are you and Buddy joining in, Andi?"

"No, just watching."

"No problem. You can keep Christine company."

Christine Wilson, the owner of the local pet store, Paws for Thought, was sitting at the far end of the room. She waved to Andi and patted the empty seat beside her.

"I'll be right over!" Andi mouthed.

Suddenly, a Jack Russell puppy came scampering into the hall on an extending leash held by a woman in her late thirties.

Andi couldn't resist going over to say hi. "He's adorable," she said, holding out her hand so the pup could sniff her.

"I know!" his owner agreed. "So's yours. Jack Russells are the best, aren't they?"

"They are," Andi said eagerly. She petted the puppy with one hand and Buddy with the other, so he wouldn't feel left out. The puppy's coat felt much softer than Buddy's because he hadn't lost all of his baby fluff yet.

Natalie joined them. "Hi, Mrs. Price. This is my friend, Andi. She's come to watch the class." She bent down to pet the puppy. "Hello, Louis. How are you?"

Louis licked her fingers, then stretched up to touch noses with Buddy.

"Okay, everyone," said Fisher, raising his voice above the chatter. "Let's get started."

"See you later, Nat," Andi said. "Good luck." She clipped on Buddy's leash and took him over to the row of chairs. "Hey, Christine."

"Hi, there. How's pet finding? Any new cases?"

"Not right now." Andi, Natalie, and their friend Tristan Saunders had formed the Pet Finders Club soon after Andi moved to Orchard Park from Florida. They'd already found lots of pets, including a pony and some reptiles that had been stolen from Christine's store. "Nobody's told *you* about any lost pets, have they?" Andi asked hopefully. She'd love to have another case to investigate.

"No. But don't worry — I know where to send them if they do. Tristan reminds me daily."

Tristan's mom was Christine's cousin, and Tris often helped out at her store.

"Okay, we're going to learn the *sit* and *stay* commands today," Fisher announced from the middle of the room. "First, get your dogs to sit."

Andi was pleased when Jet sat right away on Natalie's command. "He's definitely getting better," she whispered to Christine.

She nodded. "Fisher is a great teacher."

Unfortunately, Prince, the German shepherd, wasn't in the mood for going to school. He jumped around on the end of his leash, and it took all Jan's strength to keep him in one place. "Sit!" she shouted. At once all the dogs, including Buddy, sat down.

Everyone laughed — except for Jan. She blushed scarlet.

"Don't forget to give Prince a treat, Jan," Fisher reminded her. "It may have taken him a while, but he sat in the end and needs to be rewarded for it. Now," he went on, "I want you to tell your dogs to stay, then move a couple of steps away."

The Pekingese was the only dog to stay put when his owner, a huge man with a bushy beard, walked away. "Chester probably can't see what's going on from under all that hair," Andi whispered.

Christine grinned. "Do you think his owner should swap dogs with the woman with the German shepherd?" she joked.

In spite of the mud puddle incident on the way over, Jet was doing really well. Andi caught Natalie's eye and gave her a thumbs up.

Andi felt a draft around her feet as the door at the end of the room opened. A brown-haired man about forty years old came in and tiptoed down to the chairs. A stunning chocolate-colored collie trotted beside him on tiny, delicate paws.

The collie's owner sat down next to Andi. "Hi, are you here for Musical Freestyling?"

Andi frowned. "No, but it sounds interesting. What is it?"

The man stretched his long legs in front of him and grinned. "I guess you could call it dancing for dogs."

Andi was intrigued. "*Dancing for dogs*?"

"That's right. Just think of doing all the basic obedience movements, but with a musical soundtrack. The dogs love it."

Andi clicked her fingers, and the collie came and sat beside her. She ran her fingers through the dog's thick fur. "Brown's a really unusual color for a collie, isn't it?"

"Yes. It's pretty though, don't you think?" the man said proudly.

"She's gorgeous," Andi agreed. "What's her name?"

"Whisper. And I'm Shaun Carter."

"I'm Andi Talbot and this is Buddy." Andi bent down to smooth Bud's fur in case he was feeling left out. "I'm a member of the Pet Finders Club. You might have heard of us."

Shaun's hazel eyes lit up. "Yeah! I've seen your posters around town. I think it's great what you do. You must really love animals."

Andi nodded and gave Buddy a pet.

"Do you have time to watch the freestyling class?" Shaun went on. "I think you'd really like it."

"I'd love to!" said Andi. "Will your teacher mind having an audience?"

"I'm sure she won't, but let's ask her. That's Chloe coming in now." He stood up and waved to a tall young woman who had just slipped through the swinging doors.

Andi didn't think Chloe looked like a dog-obedience teacher. Her short, spiky hair was dyed black, and she was wearing a black denim skirt with rainbow-colored leggings underneath. A rather haughty-looking cream Pomeranian padded beside her. Chloe crept down the hall toward them, the dog's claws clicking on the floor. "Hi, Shaun. Hi, Whisper."

"This is Andi Talbot," Shaun said quietly. "Is it okay if she watches our class?"

"Sure." Chloe smiled. "The more, the merrier."

"Thanks." Andi watched as more owners and dogs crowded into the hall. The freestyling class looked very popular. "I don't suppose you've got any spaces in the class, have you?"

"I've got room for two more this semester." Chloe raised her eyebrows. "Why, are you interested?"

"I think so. It sounds like a great idea. And I'm sure my

friend Natalie would like to join, too. That's her over there with the black Lab."

"Why don't you both watch this week and see how you feel once you know what we do?" Chloe suggested.

Andi beamed at her. "We'll do that, thanks."

"That's all for today, folks," Fisher called. "Thanks for coming. And keep practicing."

Natalie raced over to Andi. "Jet did great, didn't he?"

"Yes, a big improvement! Listen, Nat, there's a dance class for dogs next. Should we stay and watch?"

"A dog dance class? Sounds cool."

Chloe went into the center of the room and smiled at the expectant circle of dogs and owners. "Hi, everyone. We'll start a new step today, called *backing*. First we'll have you moving forward while your dogs go backward, then we'll try both of you backing away from each other at the same time. Purdy and I will demonstrate." She raised her right hand and the Pomeranian pricked her ears.

Chloe crooked her finger and took a step forward, and Purdy backed away, stepping in perfect time with her owner.

"Now you try. You can use any signal — a flat hand, flicking your fingers, whatever, but it must always be the same one. And you have to keep that signal going until you want your dog to stop. We'll try it first without music."

Andi watched Shaun and Whisper closely. Shaun raised his hand, then took one pace toward Whisper. The collie stepped back, her gaze fixed on Shaun's hand. Shaun kept going forward and after a couple of moments Whisper seemed to understand what he wanted and backed in time with his steps. Andi was spellbound.

As though he could sense what she was thinking, Buddy leaned against her leg. "We'll be doing this soon, Bud," Andi told him, rubbing his chest.

"Well done, everyone," Chloe said. "Now let's try it to music." She pointed a remote control at a small stereo system, and lively pop music began to play.

Shaun and Whisper moved in time to the music, and when Shaun jauntily swung his hips, Whisper did the same. Shaun saw Andi watching and smiled.

"That's so amazing!" Andi whispered to Natalie.

"Now try the same thing facing away from your dog," Chloe instructed the class. "You just need to give the same signal behind your back. And you might like to add in some of the pivot turns we practiced last week."

Halfway through the next lesson, an alarm beeped on Shaun's cell phone.

"Sorry, Chloe, I've got to go a little early tonight," he called. "It's my turn to look after the babies." Clicking his fingers, he hurried toward the door. Whisper followed as though she were glued to her owner's heel.

"How many babies does Shaun have?" Natalie asked. "Twins? Or triplets?"

"Six," Chloe said with a smile, overhearing her.

"Six?" Andi gasped.

Chloe laughed. "Don't worry, they're not human babies. Shaun and his wife breed miniature long-haired dachshunds. One of their champions, Tooey, had puppies two weeks ago."

Natalie looked puzzled. "He's going home to look after puppies? Doesn't their mom take care of them?"

"The Carters are devoted to their dogs," Chloe explained. "They never leave new moms alone for the first few weeks."

Andi exchanged a glance with Natalie. That was the kind of pet owner they approved of! Happy, she settled down to watch the rest of the class.

Andi stuck her head around the living room door. "Hi, Mom. Can I check my e-mail please?"

"Sure, honey. Go ahead."

Andi ran up to the study with Buddy at her heels and logged on to the Internet. "As she'd hoped, there was an e-mail from Nina Nelson, who lived in Tucson, Arizona, at the Santa Rosa Crafts store. Andi had helped Nina find three semi-feral kittens while she'd been staying with her dad over the winter break.

Hi, Andi,
Things are great here. The kittens are growing soooo fast.
Dezba is turning out to be a champion curtain climber!
You can guess how much Granddad appreciates her tal-
ent. Nascha and Yas have their work cut out to keep up
with their big sister. You know how I said I'd have to let
the kittens go if they wanted to live feral like their mom?
Well, I have some <u>really</u> great news — whenever I put
them outside, they keep coming back in! It looks like they
want to live here for good — and even better, Granddad
says they can stay!

Andi hugged Buddy, picturing the three adorable kittens playing all over the busy store. She knew how much it would mean to Nina that she was able to keep them. And best of all, as far as Andi was concerned, it meant she'd be able to catch up with Dezba, Nascha, and Yas the next time she visited her dad. "This is great news, Bud!"

She quickly typed an e-mail with her congratulations and told Nina all about the Musical Freestyling class she'd watched today. Andi was really glad Shaun had invited her to stay and watch the class. It looked like so much fun! She couldn't wait to try out the moves with Bud next week. He was always surprising her with how clever he was and how quick at picking up new things. Maybe he'd be a champion dancing dog, just like Whisper!

Chapter Two

Andi was a little late arriving at school the next morning. Buddy had gotten wet on their walk after breakfast, and she'd wanted to make sure he was all dry before she left, so she hurried straight to homeroom. She stopped in the doorway, wincing at the noise her classmates were making while they waited for Mr. Dixon, their homeroom teacher, to arrive.

Andi glanced at the hamster cage in the corner of the classroom. She wondered how the newest addition to the class was handling the commotion. They'd only had Cinnamon for two weeks, and Andi hoped the little hamster wasn't trying to sleep!

She went over and peered into the cage. It had two levels linked by a metal ladder. On the lower level were an exercise wheel and a little plastic house with shredded paper spilling out of the doorway. A bowl of nuts and seeds stood beside it, and a water bottle was fastened to the bars.

There was no sign of Cinnamon, but Andi knew that hamsters sometimes buried themselves in order to feel safe and warm. She looked closer and noticed that some of the shredded paper was twitching, so she guessed he was asleep in his little house. She didn't want to disturb him so she headed for her seat.

As she squeezed past one of the other tables, Tanya McLennan flung out her arms, sending Andi's backpack flying.

"Whoa! Sorry, Andi." Tanya, a pretty girl with a small, turned-up nose, picked up the bag and handed it back. "I was just trying to show the size of the teddy bear I'm going to buy for Marie's birthday." Her green eyes sparkled with excitement.

Andi knew Tanya's little sister had been in the hospital recently for an operation on her leg. "How is Marie?" she asked.

"She's much better now," Tanya said. Some of the sparkle went out of her eyes, showing how worried she'd been. "The doctor said she can go back to school after her birthday. She's really into animals lately, so she'll totally love this stuffed bear."

"Cool," Andi said.

She had just sat down when the door swung open and Mr. Dixon backed into the room carrying two enormous white boxes. "Okay, everybody, let's quiet down," he said, setting the boxes on his desk.

Across the table from Andi, her friend Chen half stood up to get a better look at the white boxes. "What do you think he's got there?"

Andi could see better from her seat. "There's something written on the side." She craned her neck. "Treetop Hotel, Orchard Park," she read out loud. She frowned. "What would a hotel send to a school?" All she could think of were clean towels — or those miniature soaps Andi's mom collected for her when she went away on business.

"I bet Mr. Dixon's borrowed the boxes for something boring like extra notebooks," sighed Howard, who sat next to Chen.

"That's enough chatter," said Mr. Dixon. "We'll take attendance, then I have some good news for you."

"Fingers crossed we won't have to do any homework this week," whispered Chen.

"Or math is canceled," joked Larissa, who sat between Howard and Andi.

As soon as their names had all been called, Mr. Dixon lifted the lid of one of the white boxes. "I know you're all dying to know what's in here. . . ." There was more writing on the lid but it was upside down and written in swirly writing. Andi squinted, trying to figure out what it said.

"Lance Sinden, Baker," she read.

"Hey, Mr. Dixon's brought us something to eat!" Howard whispered.

"It *is* something to eat, Howard," said Mr. Dixon, who could hear like a bat when people were talking at the back of the class, "but it might not be for you. I might decide to eat all of these pastries myself." His eyes twinkled. "In fact, I might just take them down to the staff room. Teaching's a tiring job, and we need the occasional treat to keep our strength up."

The class laughed. Everyone knew he was joking.

"Lance Sinden, who used to go to this school, is the new pastry chef at The Treetop Hotel," Mr. Dixon explained, as if he had decided not to keep them in suspense any longer, "so he's had the hotel send every student a sample of his handiwork — though why they think you deserve them, I can't imagine!"

"What kind are they?" Chen called.

Mr. Dixon began to hand around the boxes. "Blueberry muffins and apricot tarts."

Andi chose an apricot tart. It was delicious, with soft

crumbly layers and just the right amount of fruity filling. "Yum," she said, licking her fingers. "I wish we could have one of these every morning!"

"Me, too," Larissa agreed.

Andi saw Natalie biting into a blueberry muffin. There were a few crumbs clinging to her cheek. Andi tried to catch her eye, but Nat was too busy eating to notice her frantic signal.

"Okay, while you're chowing down, listen up, folks. First, we'll be making a big thank-you card to send to Mr. Sinden this afternoon. Second, I want to take this time while I have your attention to tell you more about this unit's project. As you know, we're linking all of our studies with the theme of pets," Mr. Dixon said. "So, not just science or social studies, but math, English, and art, too."

"Math?" Kelly queried. "How can math fit into a pet project?"

Mr. Dixon grinned. "With a little of imagination, you'll find numbers everywhere you look! You can calculate the amount of food your pet eats in a week, a month, or a year. Or figure out how far a hamster walks on a wheel. Or how far we walk our dogs. . . ."

"I'm going to do my project on Buddy," Andi told Larissa in a low voice.

"It's great that you have a dog," Howard interrupted, "but I don't have any pets. What am I going to do my project on?"

"I'm going to use my aunt's cat," Larissa said. "Is there someone else in your family with a pet, Howard?"

Howard looked a little glum. "No."

"Anyone who doesn't have a pet," Mr. Dixon went on, as though he'd overheard, "can do their project on Cinnamon."

"Oh, great!" Howard moodily flicked his pencil across the table. "A project about a weedy little hamster!"

"He's not weedy," protested Kelly, who sat opposite Larissa. "I don't have a pet, either, and I'm going to *love* studying Cinnamon. Why don't we do our project together?" She pulled some books out of her backpack. "I've been reading up about hamsters." Howard looked a little startled when Kelly stacked the books in front of him.

"Howard, will you pass out the science sheets, please?" Mr. Dixon called.

Andi read through the questions on the sheet. The first one was: *What does your pet eat?* With Buddy, that was pretty much everything! Leftover pizza, apple cores, sandwich crusts . . .

Howard finished giving out the worksheets and

slumped down in his chair again. "Why can't I have a Rottweiler or something?" he complained.

"Come over to Cinnamon's cage," said Kelly. "We can have a look at his food dish and see exactly what's in it."

"*Boring*," Howard insisted, sliding lower in his chair.

"Come on!" Kelly grabbed his arm and dragged him to his feet. "Help me out here, Andi."

Trying not to giggle, Andi helped Kelly march Howard up to the hamster cage. Larissa came, too, pushing him from behind.

Cinnamon was out of bed now. Andi admired the pretty tan blotches on his snow-white fur, the exact color of the warm orangey spice he was named after. He was busy rearranging the wood chips that covered the cage floor.

"Hello, boy," Kelly said, letting go of Howard and bending down to look into the cage.

Cinnamon sat up on his hind legs and looked at her, his whiskers twitching.

Larissa pushed her finger through the bars of Cinnamon's cage. "Here, Cinnamon."

The hamster came to the bars and sniffed her finger, then gave it a sharp nip.

"*Ow!*" Larissa yelped, yanking her hand back.

Cinnamon leaped away from the bars as though he'd been stung and scurried into his house.

"Is Cinnamon all right?" Kelly gasped.

Andi peered through the doorway. "Yes, he's fine. He's nibbling a seed."

"What about me?" Larissa protested.

"Have you been touching any fruit?" Kelly asked, examining her friend's finger.

Larissa looked baffled. "Umm . . . maybe my apple slices. I put them in my bag just before I left this morning."

Kelly darted back to her table and returned with a book. She turned to a page that was marked with a slip of yellow paper. "It says here that hamsters have bad eyesight, so they use their sense of smell to find out what things are."

"So, Cinnamon thought Larissa's finger was a slice of apple?" Howard asked. His face brightened. "Hey, maybe hamsters aren't so boring after all!"

The rest of the week flew by. While Andi was busy working on her Buddy project, Howard got more and more excited about studying Cinnamon. Every morning, he bombarded Andi with the latest facts he had learned about hamsters. He had discovered that they came from desert areas and that they liked a sand bath to roll in, like chinchillas. Howard had decided to buy some chinchilla sand for Cinnamon in Paws for Thought.

"But people should learn how to handle him properly," he added seriously, his eyebrows knitting together in a frown. "I've seen everyone holding him way too tight. Hamsters are delicate, and it's easy to squash them."

"I guess we're all still learning about hamsters," Andi said, distracted by the math problem she was figuring out — how far she walked Buddy in a month.

"I'm going to speak to Mr. Dixon about it," Howard announced. "It's not fair to Cinnamon if people don't pick him up carefully. In fact, there are some people in this class who don't deserve to have a hamster at all."

On Monday evening, Andi and Buddy stopped by Tristan's house on their way to the Musical Freestyling class. "Come in," he said, opening the door. "I just have to feed Lucy." He grabbed a can of cat food and forked some into her bowl. "Lucy!" he called, setting the bowl down on her mat in the corner of the kitchen.

"Come on," Andi said. "I don't want to be late to my first class."

"Almost ready. Lucy! Dinner!"

There was no sign of his pretty tabby cat. "Hang on, I'll see if she's upstairs." Tristan raced up the stairs.

Andi heard him going from room to room, calling.

"Tris!" she yelled.

Tristan ran down again. "She must be out in the yard." He darted to the back door and flung it open. "Lucy! Dinner!"

"I'll go without you," Andi warned.

"There she is!" Lucy was sitting on a raised wooden deck, half-hidden behind a huge flowerpot. "Come on, girl. Aren't you cold sitting out here?"

Lucy stood up and stretched before padding calmly toward Tristan. He scooped her up, carried her into the house and set her down by her bowl. "I'm ready now," he said, washing his hands.

"About time." Andi glanced at her watch. The class was due to start in ten minutes. "We'll have to run."

As they sprinted across the parking lot outside the ASPCA, Andi saw Shaun arriving with Whisper. "Hi, Shaun," she called. "How are the babies?"

Beside her, Tristan looked puzzled, but Shaun grinned. "They're great, actually. Thanks for asking."

Then, taking pity on Tristan's baffled expression, Andi explained who the "babies" were.

"Whoa! I bet miniature dachshund puppies are really cute," he said. "I've never seen one before."

"That's easily fixed," said Shaun. "You guys are welcome to come see them sometime."

"Really?" Andi beamed.

"If it's okay with your parents, you can come anytime." Shaun wrote down his address and gave it to Andi.

"Could we come tomorrow after school?" Tristan asked hopefully.

"Sounds perfect," Shaun replied.

"Awesome!" Andi said as they went into the hall.

They arrived just as the Basic Obedience class ended. "Jet's done really well today, Natalie," Fisher Pearce was saying.

The Labrador barked and wagged his tail as if he were glad Fisher had noticed.

Chloe arrived and Andi found a space near Natalie to work in. "This is going to be great!" she said excitedly. Tristan gave them a thumbs-up from the chairs at the end of the room.

"Hi, everyone," said Chloe. "Welcome to Andi and Buddy, and Natalie and Jet, our newest students." Everyone smiled warmly at the two girls. Chloe continued, "We're going to practice backing again today."

After a bit of instruction from Chloe, Andi raised her hand and crooked her finger like she had seen in the previous class. Buddy jumped up to lick her hand.

"No, Bud," Andi said. "That's the signal for backing. You have to walk away from me." She took a step forward and Buddy jumped up again, his tail wagging.

Andi laughed. "Let's watch Whisper for a bit," she said.

Buddy sat beside her and they watched Whisper back across the hall, keeping in time with Shaun's steps.

"That's how it's done, Bud." Andi faced Buddy again and made the backing signal.

Buddy glanced at Whisper, then stepped back.

"That's it!" Andi exclaimed. She stepped forward and Buddy took another pace back. He kept looking across at Whisper, as if he wanted to make sure he was doing it properly.

"Buddy's a natural," Shaun praised. "He seems to have a real feel for the beat."

Andi beamed. "Thanks! I think he's learned from watching Whisper."

At the end of the class, Andi and Natalie hurried over to speak to Tristan. "What did you think?" Andi demanded.

Tristan shrugged. "Not bad. Maybe I should bring Lucy next week. She's got great musical taste. Every time my mom plays one of her CDs, Lucy runs out of the room!"

Andi laughed.

"Bye, guys!" called Shaun. "See you tomorrow."

"What did he mean?" said Natalie.

"He's invited us to see Tooey's puppies tomorrow," Andi explained.

"Whoa!" Natalie exclaimed. "We're meeting so many new dogs now, I'm starting to feel like I might grow fur and a tail!"

Chapter Three

Andi's mom wanted to go with the Pet Finders to meet Shaun and the miniature dachshunds, so she picked them up after school and drove them over. A sports car was parked in the driveway and there was a bird feeder hanging in a tree near the front door. A few birds were feeding, but they flew away as the Pet Finders approached.

"Six puppies," Natalie breathed as she rang the doorbell. "I can't wait to see them."

"Me neither," Andi agreed. She'd been thinking about them all day at school and had gotten called on twice while not paying attention.

Mrs. Talbot laughed. "I remember all the things Buddy got up to when he was a puppy. Imagine having six little bundles of mischief!"

Shaun Carter opened the door with Whisper at his heels. "Come in! I'm glad you could make it."

Andi introduced her mom, who smiled and shook hands with Shaun. Then he led them into a spacious living room lined with windows reaching from floor to ceiling. A library of dog books filled a bookcase on the far side of the room, and the mantelpiece was crammed with photos of miniature dachshund puppies.

"Eleanor, my wife, isn't here, so it's just me and Whisper dog-sitting this afternoon," Shaun explained. Tooey and her pups were lying in a wooden dog bed in a patch of winter sunlight. A bowl of water stood nearby.

Tooey was an adorable cylinder of silky chocolate-and-black hair, with long floppy ears edged with a velvety soft fringe. She lifted her head as the Pet Finders came in, and her plumy cocoa-colored tail began to wag. Six puppies, like tiny balls of fluff, were snuggled around her. Andi crept toward them, not wanting to frighten them by moving too quickly.

Natalie and Tristan followed. "They're so cute!" Andi whispered.

The Pet Finders kneeled beside the dog bed while Mrs. Talbot sat down in a nearby armchair. "How old are they?" Natalie asked.

"Two weeks, so their eyes are open now and they sometimes get out of the basket and have a sniff around," Shaun said. "But not for long. They like being with their mom."

Andi let Tooey sniff her hand, then gently touched the nearest pup; it was mostly black with a chocolate chest and tail. It rubbed its head against her hand and gave a shrill bark. It reminded Andi of the first time she'd seen Buddy. He'd been a little bigger than these pups, but he'd been just as cute and fluffy, and he'd had a way of looking up at Andi with his sweet brown eyes that made her pick him up and hug him.

Natalie turned to Shaun. "Is it okay to hold one?"

"Sure," Shaun replied. "It's good for them to be handled. It helps them get used to people."

"Come on, little one." Natalie slid her hand underneath one of the puppies and lifted her up. "You're a little beauty, aren't you? Oh!" She broke off in surprise. "Her tummy's cream. I've never seen a cream dachshund before."

"Good call," said Shaun. "It's a very rare color, but the puppies' father, Snowy, is pure cream." He pointed to the sofa, and Andi saw another dachshund curled up there. At first she thought he was asleep, but then she noticed that he had one eye slightly open. *He's watching out for the puppies*, she thought, *to make sure we don't hurt them.*

"All but one of the puppies have some cream on them," Shaun said.

"How many boys and how many girls are there?" Tristan asked, picking up a puppy with black-edged ears. He stroked its head, and the puppy licked his fingers with a tiny, pink tongue.

"Four girls and two boys," Shaun told him.

"Have you thought of names for them yet?" said Andi. She laughed as one of the puppies tumbled out of the dog bed, turned head-over-heels, and stood up, its eyes wide with surprise.

"Not yet. Since we're breeding show dogs, naming them is pretty important. We usually raise about five or six pups a year, and it's hard coming up with good show names for all of them." He grinned. "You'd be amazed at how long their names have to be, considering they're such tiny puppies! For example, Tooey's real name is Bluebell Lady Twoshoes, because she came from the Rose Kennels. All their puppy names begin with flowers."

"Do you have a theme for your dogs' names?" said Tristan.

Shaun nodded. "American states. All these pups' names will start with Vermont."

"How about Vermont Sugar for the puppy with the most cream fur?" Natalie suggested.

"And Vermont Hershey Bar for the chocolate brown boy," Tristan added.

Shaun laughed. "Well, maybe not. We like to find names that sound pretty impressive. Snowy's really called Montana Snow Tiger! But we also like to be able to shorten them to something a little more family-friendly."

Andi looked at Tristan and Natalie. "Do you remember the last time we tried to name a puppy?"

"Yes!" Natalie said. "That little yellow Labrador we found by the freeway! She was so sweet."

"I haven't seen Mike forever," Tristan mused. "I wonder how the puppy is."

The Pet Finders had saved the Labrador puppy's life when she'd been abandoned on the outskirts of Orchard Park. She'd been adopted by the local mailman, Mike Morgan.

"I wonder what Mike called her in the end," Tristan added.

"Probably not Fang," said Natalie, reminding them all of Tristan's comical suggestions.

Tristan shrugged. "Okay, that wasn't one of my better

ideas." He looked at the puppies. "Hey, I wonder if any of these guys have sharp teeth."

"No, Tristan!" Natalie said sharply. "No Fangs here, either. Or Bruisers. Or any other name that sounds mean."

Shaun smiled. "I agree. We don't want to make our dogs sound hostile, even though dachshunds are famous for being brave in spite of their size. You know, I once heard of a miniature dachshund that took on a bull when its owner fell over in a field."

"Did the dog win?" Tristan asked, impressed.

"It managed to draw the bull away and give its owner time to get up and out of the field. The dog escaped under the fence, so I guess you could say it won."

"How about Vermont Brave Heart, then?" Tristan suggested. "Or Vermont Heroic Hunter?"

"Heroic Hunter," Shaun echoed. "That one's pretty good. And the puppy could be Hero for short. We'll have to see which one is bravest."

Andi leaned over the dog bed to pet the other puppies. There were two black-and-cream puppies playfully nipping each other's paws, and a chocolate-colored puppy lying curled up beside his mother. His eyes were shut tight, as though he were determined to sleep through his sisters' game. Andi ran her finger down his velvety-soft back. "Do you know, the way this one's lying all curled up reminds me of this image I saw everywhere in artwork when I was in Arizona. It was this hunch-backed flute-playing god named . . ." Andi thought hard for a moment. "Kokopelli!"

"Kokopelli," repeated Natalie. "That sounds cool."

Andi stroked the puppy's tiny ears. "Maybe he could be called Vermont Kokopelli."

"And Koko for short," Tristan said. "That sounds pretty chocolaty to match his brown fur."

"Vermont Kokopelli," Shaun repeated. "You know, I think that name really suits him."

Andi felt a little thrill. She'd named a puppy! She grinned at her mom.

"Good job," Judy Talbot said, smiling back.

The puppy woke up and lifted his head. "He knows we're talking about him," Natalie said.

The puppy sat up and put his front paws on Andi's hand. He didn't look like the hunch-backed flute-playing god now, but he was still adorable. She lifted him onto her lap. "Hello, Koko. What do you think of your new name?"

Koko licked Andi's finger with his pink tongue, then gave a high-pitched bark. Andi laughed. "I think he likes it."

The puppy closed his front paws around Andi's thumb as though they were tiny hands. He shook his head, making his silky ears flap, then rolled over with his tail wagging furiously.

Andi rubbed his tummy. "Hey!" she said, peering closer. "This little black patch on his tummy is shaped just like a keyhole!" She traced around it with her finger while Koko wriggled happily.

"Are you going to keep any of the puppies?" Natalie asked Shaun.

"No, they're all for sale. Eleanor has posted a photo of the litter on our website. We've had lots of congratulatory messages from other breeders, thanks to these five puppies with cream in their coats. Everyone likes the rare colors! But we're in no hurry to sell them, so we've got plenty of time to find the best homes."

"How do you decide who'd make a good owner?" Tristan wanted to know.

"Well, it's great if they've owned dogs before, especially dachshunds. We never let our dogs go to anyone who doesn't know a little something about the breed. And they need to understand how much commitment it takes to be a dog owner."

"It sounds like applying for a job," Tristan joked.

"It is," Shaun agreed. "A full-time, twenty-four/seven job."

The door opened and a slim woman with a heart-shaped face and a dimpled smile came in carrying two bulging bags of groceries. "Phew!" she exclaimed, setting them down. "Better than a workout at the gym!"

"This is my wife, Eleanor," said Shaun. "Eleanor, this is Judy Talbot." He gestured toward Andi's mom who stood up and shook hands with Eleanor. "And this is Andi, Tristan, and Natalie."

"Hi, there," said Eleanor smiling. "I'm honored to have such famous pet detectives in my home. And eager to hear what you think about our own puppies, of course."

"They're gorgeous," Andi said. She rubbed Koko's tummy again, and he wrinkled his nose at her.

"We've named this little chap," Shaun said, pointing to Koko. "Vermont Kokopelli. Or Koko if you prefer."

Eleanor's green eyes shone. "Nice one!"

"Andi thought of it," Shaun told her. He glanced at his watch. "I'd better get going. I've got a volleyball game in twenty minutes. Stop by again, guys. Anytime!" And with that, he shot out of the room.

"Are you all okay here while I go and change?" Eleanor asked.

"You bet!" Tristan said.

"Great! We don't like to leave them on their own, but I'm sure they'll be fine with you."

When Eleanor had left the room, Tristan picked up one of the puppies — a girl with more cream on her than the others — and let her snuggle against his chest. "It's amazing that Shaun and Eleanor never leave the puppies alone." He grinned. "It doesn't sound like the Pet Finders will be needed around here any time soon."

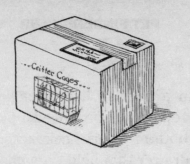

Chapter Four

Andi thought about Tooey's puppies as she walked to school the next morning, picturing the way Koko kept rolling over to have his tummy rubbed. She'd have to e-mail Nina and tell her she'd named a purebred show puppy, and that the name was inspired by her trip to Tucson.

During homeroom that morning, Andi joined her friends at Cinnamon's cage.

"I've brought him some chunks of carrot," Howard said, opening his backpack and pulling out some books about hamsters and a very crumpled homework sheet.

"Are you still doing hamster research, Howard?" Andi asked, leafing through one of the books.

Howard nodded. "Did you know that hamsters need a block of wood to gnaw on, to keep their teeth from growing too much? I'm going to buy Cinnamon one on

Saturday." With a flourish like a magician whisking a rabbit out of a top hat, he produced a plastic bag of carrots from the bottom of his backpack. "Here it is." He put it into the drawer that held Cinnamon's food.

"Who's going to feed him today?" Natalie asked, taking charge.

"We should make a schedule," Howard suggested, "so everyone can have a turn. Otherwise, we'll just argue about it." He shot Kelly a glance. "*Some* people have already had two turns while the rest of us haven't even had one."

"You can count me out," said Larissa. "I'm not going anywhere near that hamster." She still had a bandage on the finger Cinnamon had bitten.

"He won't bite you again," Andi said. "It was only because your hands smelled like an apple."

"You can help me," said Howard. He grinned. "I'll do all the dangerous stuff and you can refill the water bottle."

"Okay. But I am *not* putting my fingers inside the cage again."

Mr. Dixon told everyone to sit down. "A schedule is a good idea," he agreed. "Everyone write your name on a piece of paper while I take attendance. Afterward, we'll draw names to see who gets to take care of Cinnamon today."

He collected the pieces of paper and put them in a tin, then pulled one out. "Today, Tanya will be in charge of Cinnamon," he announced.

Andi was disappointed that she hadn't been picked. She waited hopefully as Mr. Dixon drew out the name for the next day. "I hope it's me," Howard whispered.

"Robert," Mr. Dixon said, reading the next slip of paper. He went on drawing names until everyone in the class had been assigned a day with Cinnamon. Andi was in charge next Friday, the day after Larissa.

"I'm not sure I want to do this!" Larissa groaned.

"Don't worry," Howard said. "I'll give you a hand." He beamed. "That way I get two turns. And Cinnamon will have two days of being held by someone who knows not to squeeze him."

"Thanks, Howard." Larissa turned to Andi then. "How's your Buddy project going?"

"It's not exactly about Buddy anymore."

"What are you doing it on, then?"

"It's a secret." Since she'd started Musical Freestyling classes, Andi had changed her mind about the subject of her project. She'd decided to call it *Talented Pets* now.

Buddy would still be the star, of course, but Andi planned to include photos of Whisper, too. The highlight of the project would be a video of her and Bud doing their freestyling routine, and she was spending every spare minute practicing. Remembering what Mr. Dixon had said about including math in her project, she was planning to figure out how much it would cost if she took Buddy to freestyling classes for six months, nine months, and a whole year. And for English class, she was writing a poem called *Dancing Dogs*.

"You can tell *us* what it's about," Howard said. "We won't say a word."

Andi shook her head. "No way! You'll have to wait and see."

The bell rang. "Time for gym class," Mr. Dixon said.

Andi snatched up her backpack and darted to the door: Gym was her favorite class. As she ran into the corridor, she collided with Tanya McLennan.

"Look where you're going!" Tanya snapped as her backpack skidded along the corridor.

"Sorry," Andi panted. She began to pick up Tanya's books and pens.

"Me, too." Tanya said, looking a little stressed out.

Andi glanced at Tanya in surprise. "Are you okay?"

Tanya shrugged. "I guess."

Andi could see there was something wrong. "Can I do anything to help?"

"Not unless you provide a teddy bear–finding service, too!"

Andi finished picking up Tanya's things and put them into her backpack. "Problem with Marie's birthday gift?"

Tanya nodded miserably. "The toy store's sold out of the teddy bear I had in mind. The rest are all so plain."

They reached the locker rooms. "Well," Andi said, hanging her backpack on her peg. "There are plenty of other stuffed animals out there. Or, what about a toy farm?"

Tanya shook her head. "Mom gets mad about little plastic animals all over the place, so that's out." She shrugged. "Don't worry, I'll think of something. But let me know if you come up with any good ideas, okay?"

For the next few days, Andi practiced freestyling with Buddy whenever she could. She worked hard on her poem, too. She was already halfway through and, when it was all written, she planned to type it into the computer, print it out, and decorate it with drawings of Buddy, Whisper, and Jet dancing.

On Saturday afternoon, Andi, Tristan, and Natalie met near school to take Buddy and Jet for a walk in the park.

It was a bright day, but the wind was cold and Andi tied her scarf tighter as they set off along the road. "Do you mind if we go a different way?" Tristan asked. "My mom and dad are selling some new apartments on Stanbury Road and I'd like to have a look at them. They sound really cool!"

"Sure," Andi agreed. Tristan's parents ran a real estate business.

"As long as it's not miles out of the way," Natalie warned.

"It's not much farther," Tristan said.

While they walked, Tristan told them about the new baby hamsters that had just arrived at Paws for Thought. "They're so cute," he said. "Really tiny and fluffy."

Suddenly they heard paws racing toward them, and a gorgeous yellow face leaped up to greet Andi.

"Hey, girl!" Andi exclaimed. It was the rescued Labrador that Mike the mailman had adopted. Andi crouched down, and the young dog jumped up and planted her feet on Andi's knees. "You remember me, don't you. What a clever girl!" Andi praised her.

The Labrador barked, then jumped up at Natalie and Tristan, her feathery tail wagging furiously.

"It's so good to see you again!" said Tristan, ruffling her ears. "You look great!"

Buddy and Jet leaped around the young dog, barking with excitement.

Mike jogged around the corner. "Hey, guys, how are you?" His mailbag was bouncing on his hip, and he was carrying a large, rectangular package under his arm.

"Hey!" Tristan replied. "Where have you been? We haven't seen you in ages."

"I took a few weeks off for some high-altitude training in the Rockies. It was amazing! And Lucky loved it, too."

"Lucky? Is that her name?" Andi was so pleased to hear the beautiful dog had a name at last.

"It's perfect!" said Tristan.

"Totally," Nat agreed. "Why didn't we think of that one?"

At the mention of her name, Lucky tried to climb right onto Andi's lap, but she was so excited that she scrabbled too far and fell off the other side, landing on Natalie's feet.

"Make sure you don't scratch Nat's shoes," Tristan warned the dog. "Or you'll be in big trouble."

"Oh, she's cute enough to get away with *anything*," said Natalie. She ran her fingers through the puppy's soft yellow coat. "She's in great shape, Mike."

"Thanks," said Mike. "She's good company, too. I can't imagine what it would be like not to have her around all the time. There's just one problem with taking her marathon training — she's better at it than I am!"

Andi laughed. "She's got four legs. You've got only two." She straightened up. "Do you want a hand with that?" she asked, nodding toward the box he was holding.

"Don't worry, it's not heavy. According to the label, it's a *critter cage*. Empty, I hope!" He grinned and checked the address. "Actually, it's for this house right here."

Andi noticed the name on the package. "Hey! It's for Tanya McLennan. She's in my class. We can deliver it for you."

"Perfect, thanks. I've promised Lucky a five-mile run as soon as I've finished up, and I can tell she's itching to get going!"

He handed the box to Andi. As he had said, it wasn't heavy, just bulky, with rather sharp edges that dug into her hip. She was glad she had to carry it only as far as Tanya's front door.

They said goodbye to Mike and Lucky, making one last fuss over the gorgeous little dog, and headed up the path. The house was modern and it looked roomy, with tall front windows.

Natalie rang the bell. "I hope she invites us in to look at her critter," she said.

Tanya opened the door. "Uh, hi," she said, obviously surprised to see them.

"We're just delivering this for the mailman," Andi told her, handing it over. "It's an animal cage. I didn't know you had a pet, Tanya."

"It's for a mouse," she said quickly.

"A mouse! Can we see it?" Tristan asked.

"No, sorry. I don't have it yet. But thanks for delivering the cage. Bye!" Tanya put the box on the floor and shut the door.

Andi frowned as the door closed. "Wow, she really is in a hurry!"

Natalie shrugged. "Well, at least we helped out Mike. And it was great to see Lucky again! Now we know her name," she said with a smile.

They set back off along the sidewalk.

"I wonder why Tanya didn't buy the cage at Paws for Thought," Tristan mused. "She must have had to pay a lot of postage by buying it through mail order."

"Never mind," Natalie said. "How much farther is it to these apartments, Tris? They are in Orchard Park, aren't they?"

Book Signing

Meet Dale Savage

Author of *Pet Wolf*

Chapter Five

To Andi's disappointment, Shaun and Whisper missed the next freestyling class. Andi was sure Buddy was disappointed, too — he kept looking around for his dance partner the whole time he and Andi practiced their moves. When Andi asked Chloe if Shaun was okay, the instructor explained that he'd had to stay home because someone had arranged to see Tooey's puppies. Andi felt a pang of excitement that one of the gorgeous little dogs might be about to find a brilliant home. She hoped Koko put on a good show for the prospective buyer!

Heading home after the class, Andi and Natalie passed a sign in the window of the bookstore on Main Street. "Oh, wow!" Andi said, stopping so abruptly that Buddy jerked on the end of his leash. "Dale Savage is doing a book signing!"

Dale Savage was the host of her favorite TV show, *The Wolf at Home*. It explained the natural behavior of dogs, showing how all their habits were based on survival instincts from their wild past. Andi had been fascinated to learn that Buddy chased after balls and sticks because he had the same deeply rooted instinct that his wolf ancestors had needed to catch food by running after it.

"I can't wait to read his new book, *Pet Wolf!*" said Natalie. "His show is fantastic! Do you know why Jet turns around in his basket before he goes to sleep?" She didn't wait for Andi to answer. "It's because ancient dogs had to circle to flatten the grass they wanted to sleep on."

"Buddy does that, too," Andi said, thinking about the way he turned and turned on the spot before settling into the crook of her legs every night when they went to bed.

"Jet used to do it on my lap when he was a puppy," Natalie said. "I wouldn't want him sitting on me now, I'd be squashed!" She patted him. "But you can sit *beside* me any time, boy."

They walked past the road where the Carters lived, and Andi hesitated. "Do you think we could call in and see if any of the puppies have found a new home?"

"Sure," said Natalie. She glanced at Andi. "You'll really miss Koko if he's sold, won't you?"

"I guess," Andi admitted. "But he deserves to have a really special owner all to himself."

Shaun Carter opened the door. "Oh, hi. I thought you might be the guy who's coming to look at the puppies. He's running late, but Eleanor's home in time to meet him." He frowned. "We weren't expecting to see you today, were we?"

"No," said Andi. "But Chloe told us that someone was coming to see the puppies, and I wanted to know how the visit went."

Shaun grinned. "Checking to make sure Koko gets a good owner, hmm? Come on in. Buddy and Jet will have to wait in the kitchen, though. I'm afraid the puppies haven't had their vaccinations yet."

Jet flopped down beside the stove and Buddy went to lap from Whisper's water bowl. "We'll be right back," Andi promised as she shut the door.

Eleanor was in the sitting room, kneeling on the floor beside the dog basket. "Hi, there," she said, shifting over so they could join her.

"Hi," said Andi. "Thanks for letting us see the puppies again." She crouched down and laughed as Koko gently nibbled her finger then shook his head, making his ears flap.

Eleanor smiled. "It's easy to see which one's your favorite!"

"And I love this little one best," said Natalie. She lifted up the chocolate-and-cream girl. "Have you chosen a name for her yet?"

Eleanor nodded. "Vermont Maple Leaf. Leaf for short."

"Leaf," Natalie echoed. "It's perfect!"

Eleanor glanced at the clock. "I hope this guy's coming. He sounds perfect." She fetched a sheet of paper from the table. "Want to see the photos of the dachshunds he used to own?"

Andi admired the two images on the printout. One was a sleek black-and-tan, long-haired dachshund gazing straight into the camera, while the other picture showed a smooth-coated fawn dachshund with a paler neck and tummy. Both looked fit and healthy.

The doorbell rang. Shaun went to answer it and came back with a friendly looking man in his early twenties. He had red hair, warm blue eyes, and a broad smile. "Hi, there. You must be Mrs. Carter." He shook hands with Eleanor. "I'm Zan Kirby. Thanks so much for letting me see the puppies. Is it possible for me to meet their mom and dad, too, and have a look at your whole set-up? The best way to tell how a pup will turn out is to see how its parents are cared for, I always say."

"Absolutely!" Shaun Carter agreed. "It makes my blood boil the way some people buy dogs from puppy farms without a thought for the animals' welfare."

Andi and Natalie put the puppies gently back into the basket and stood up to make room for Zan Kirby. "Thanks," he said. "Are you two choosing a puppy? You look a little young. Shouldn't your mom and dad be here with you?"

"We're just friends," Natalie explained.

"Oh, I see." Zan let Tooey sniff his hand before he tried to touch any of the pups.

Well, he certainly knows about dogs, Andi thought approvingly.

"He's a cute little fella," Zan commented, picking up Koko. The puppy snuggled against his chest, wagging his tail. Then he reached out and held Zan's thumb with his front paws, just as he'd done with Andi's.

Zan laughed. "I've never known a dog to do that before."

Andi was thrilled Zan had picked out her favorite. She watched him gently check Koko over, looking at his eyes and teeth.

"He seems healthy. And his teeth are sharp enough!" Zan added as Koko gave him a playful nip.

"You know the puppies won't be ready to leave us until they're eight weeks old and have had their first shots?" Eleanor Carter checked. "I've already booked their appointment with Dr. Harvey. You can check the exact date on our website if you like."

Zan nodded. "But I'll need to pay you a deposit to reserve the puppy I'm interested in, right?"

"Yes."

Zan set Koko down on the floor and watched as the puppy tried to clamber onto his lap. "He's a determined little one. That's good. It's a nice quality in a dog." He picked Koko up again. "I'd like a little more time before I make up my mind. Would it be okay to come again to make sure this little guy and I are right for each other?"

"Sure," said Shaun. He glanced at Eleanor, and Andi could tell they were impressed.

Zan put Koko back in the basket. "Thanks again," he said, standing up. "I'll see you soon." He shook hands with Shaun and Eleanor, smiled at Andi and Natalie, and headed for the door.

"We should go, too," said Natalie. "Thanks for letting us see the puppies again."

"Anytime! It's good for the puppies to meet lots of

new people." Eleanor reached down to pet Leaf's head. "Zan looks like he'd be a fantastic owner, but it's a shame we can't keep them all!"

On Thursday, it was Larissa's turn to take care of Cinnamon. During homeroom, Howard got the cage and set it down on Andi's table. "You change the water, Larissa, and I'll do everything else."

"I won't have to put my hand in the cage?" Larissa said, eyeing it anxiously.

"Nope. Super Howard will risk life and limb by changing Cinnamon's bedding and topping off his food bowl!" Howard zoomed across the room to get the new bedding, with one arm stretched out in front of him like Superman. Andi laughed. Such a comedian!

The shredded paper rustled, and Cinnamon peeped out of his little house. "Who wants to hold him while I change his bedding?" Howard asked, returning with a bag of shredded paper. "Only people who know how to hold hamsters properly need apply."

"I'll do it!" Andi offered. She held out her hands as Howard dumped the bag of bedding on the table and tried to open the cage door. "Ouch!" he said, pulling his hand away.

"Did he bite you, too?" Larissa asked nervously.

"No. I caught my finger in the door. It's really stiff."

"We should get it fixed," said Tanya McLennan, coming over to see what was going on. "It would be awful if Cinnamon got stuck in there."

"Maybe the janitor could do it," Andi suggested.

"Good idea," Tanya agreed.

"Yeah. I'll ask him at lunchtime." Howard yanked the door open and reached into the cage. Cinnamon climbed happily onto Howard's hand so he could be lifted out. Kelly had been in charge of taming the hamster. To start, she'd put a cup into the cage and let Cinnamon climb inside. Then she'd lifted him and the cup out and given him a slice of carrot to tempt him onto her hand. Now, he was tame enough not to need the cup anymore — he climbed straight onto anyone's hand when it appeared inside his cage.

Howard held his hand next to Andi's then, and Cinnamon stepped across. The little hamster sat up on his hind legs and washed his whiskers, gazing at Andi with his beady black eyes.

Andi stroked his tan-and-white fur with one finger. He felt soft and warm. "He's so cute!" she murmured. "Don't you even want to pet him, Larissa?"

Larissa made a face. "No, thanks! Hamsters are definitely *not* my favorite animals. But that doesn't mean I'll let him get thirsty." She unclipped Cinnamon's water bottle and went to the sink to refill it.

"He's really tame now," Tanya said. "He'll come to anyone." She held out a sunflower seed and the hamster took it in his tiny paws, then tucked it into his pouch.

When the cage had been cleaned out, Andi put Cinnamon back inside. He crawled straight inside his house, rearranging the bedding with his teeth as he went.

"Time for history," Mr. Dixon announced.

Larissa closed the cage, and Howard carried it back to the corner. "There you go, Cinnamon." He glanced at the clock. "Hey, guys, can you remind me that I've got a dentist appointment today? My mom's picking me up at ten-thirty, and I forgot the last one."

Andi rolled her eyes. "Typical!"

"I'm just glad you didn't have to go before we'd cleaned the cage," Larissa said seriously. "Thanks for helping me."

At the end of the day, Andi went back to her classroom to get her math homework. Larissa was with her, telling Andi about how hard it was to sculpt her aunt's cat in clay for the art portion of her pet project.

In the classroom, Chen and Kelly were leaning over Cinnamon's cage.

"Is Cinnamon awake?" Andi asked.

"We can't see him. He must be curled up in bed," said Kelly.

"He's probably waiting for Howard," Chen joked. He peered closer and frowned. "Normally, his bedding moves a tiny bit when he's asleep, but it's completely still."

Andi hurried over, suddenly feeling anxious. She opened the cage and tapped the side of the house. "Cinnamon! Cinnamon?" She was reluctant to wake him up if he was having a nap, but she wanted to be sure he was okay before she went home.

There was still no movement.

Andi shifted the paper so she could see right inside the house. "He's not there!" she said in alarm.

Larissa's face turned white and she sat down heavily on a chair.

"What's up?" asked Natalie, coming into the classroom.

"Cinnamon's gone!" Andi exclaimed. She raised her voice to make herself heard as more people came in to collect their backpacks before going home. "Listen, everyone. Cinnamon's missing. We'll all have to search the classroom."

"Slowly and carefully," Natalie added. "We don't want to scare him."

"We need to look in our bags," Andi went on. "Hamsters are pretty good at climbing, so even if your bag hasn't been on the floor, he might have found a way into it."

"And we need to look in cabinets and underneath everything," Natalie instructed.

Everyone began to search, tipping out school bags, peering under radiators, and looking into all the closets. "We don't know much about finding tiny indoor pets," Andi whispered to Natalie as they lay down flat to check under the bookcase. All their classmates knew that she, Natalie, and Tristan were the Pet Finders, and they'd be relying on them to find the little hamster. Andi hated the thought of letting them down.

"I think I can see him!" Chen shouted from the back of the room. "He's under this cabinet."

Andi and Natalie hurried over, but before they reached him, Chen groaned. "False alarm. It's a ball of orange wool." He held it up. "Must be from our macramé unit last term."

With everyone helping, it didn't take long to search the room. But Cinnamon was nowhere to be seen.

"What do we do now?" Chen asked. Everyone turned to Andi and Natalie expectantly.

"I'm not sure," Andi admitted. "We've never had to find a missing hamster before."

"But we did find a guinea pig, so it can't be too much harder," noted Nat. "Let me check the hamster sites I bookmarked," Kelly said. She ran to the computer desk and logged on.

Andi and Natalie looked over her shoulder as she brought up a hamster website. It said that escaped hamsters usually found a place to hide until nighttime. "Lost hamsters often come out and wander around when it gets dark," Andi read.

"That's no help," said Chen. "We won't be here to catch Cinnamon then."

With a start, Andi saw that Larissa was still sitting at their table with her hands over her face. Her shoulders were shaking, and Andi realized she was crying. She went over and put her arm round Larissa. "Don't worry. We'll find him. He couldn't have gone far."

Larissa just shook her head and carried on crying. Andi couldn't help feeling a bit surprised by Larissa's reaction — after all, she was hardly Cinnamon's biggest fan.

Natalie was reading a website over Kelly's shoulder. "Look, we can make a trap!" she said. "A gentle one," she added when someone gasped. "The website shows you what to do."

Mr. Dixon came in. "What's going on? Love school so much you can't bear to go home?"

"Cinnamon's gone," Natalie told him.

His smile faded. "Oh, no. We'll have to organize a search."

"We've already done that," said Andi. "But Kelly found a website with some tips on how to catch escaped hamsters." She squeezed Larissa's arm, then stood up so she could see the computer screen, too.

"First we need a bucket," said Kelly, running her finger down the list of tips on the screen.

Mr. Dixon sent Chen to ask the janitor for one.

"We'll need wood shavings from Cinnamon's cage," Natalie continued. "And some food."

"And books," Kelly added.

"Books?" echoed Robert. "For Cinnamon to read?"

Nobody laughed. Looking around, Andi saw she was surrounded by worried faces.

"The books will make a staircase up to the top of the bucket," Kelly explained.

By the time Chen came back with the bucket, the

books had been piled up. He did as Kelly said, and put the bucket beside the books, though from his puzzled expression it was clear he didn't know what was going on.

"Now, Nat, you need to tip the wood shavings into the bucket and scatter some food on top," Kelly went on. "Hopefully Cinnamon will smell the food and wood shavings," she explained. "It should remind him of home, so he'll climb up the books and drop into the bucket."

"Excellent!" Chen exclaimed. "He'll never get out of there! That's a great website you found, Kelly."

"Now that the trap's set up, can someone tell me what happened?" said Mr. Dixon.

"Cinnamon must have escaped while we were out of the room," Andi told him. "His cage was empty when we came back from our last class." She showed Mr. Dixon the cage door. "It's really stiff, but I'm sure nobody would have left it undone. . . ." She trailed off, remembering Larissa's reaction to Cinnamon's disappearance. Andi looked around for her, wondering if she could have left the cage open by mistake, but Larissa wasn't there. "That's weird," she remarked to Natalie. "Larissa's gone already."

"Huh?" Natalie raised her eyebrows. "Considering Cinnamon was her responsibility today, you'd think she could have stayed to help with the trap."

"Maybe she had an appointment after school," Andi said. She really hoped Larissa hadn't left the cage door open, but it would definitely explain why she seemed so upset. From the look on Nat's face, she was obviously thinking the same thing.

The class repacked their bags and cleaned up quickly. "I hope we find him," Andi said as she and Natalie walked out of school. She shivered, remembering the time she'd lost Buddy when she'd first moved to Orchard Park. She'd been worried sick. And poor Cinnamon was so much tinier and more helpless than Buddy. "Let's hope that trap works," she said, crossing her fingers for luck.

"I'll call Tristan when I get home and tell him what's going on," Natalie said. "He's a Pet Finder, so he should be involved."

They reached the end of her road. "See you tomorrow!" Andi called, hitching her backpack onto her shoulder. Wherever Cinnamon was, she hoped the cute little hamster had found a safe, snug corner for the night.

Chapter Six

"You're quiet, Andi," Mrs. Talbot said, while Andi was feeding Buddy that evening. "What's up?"

"I keep thinking about Cinnamon."

Her mom patted her arm. "He'll be okay. It's pretty common for hamsters to escape, and they usually turn up the next day. I bet he'll be in that bucket when you get to school tomorrow."

Andi forced a smile.

"Are you going to practice your freestyle later?" said Mrs. Talbot.

Andi shook her head. "I don't feel like practicing tonight. Is it okay if I e-mail Dad to tell him about Cinnamon?" He was pretty interested in the Pet Finders Club since he'd helped her find Nina's kittens in Tucson.

"Sure, honey."

Andi ran upstairs with Buddy at her heels. He lay

across her feet as soon as she sat down at the computer. He seemed subdued, as though he could sense Andi's anxiety. And she *was* worried. It was strange to be working on the case of a missing pet that she had known so well.

She typed quickly, telling her dad about Cinnamon's disappearance. Then she described the new dachshund friends she'd made. Since she didn't have a picture of Tooey's puppies, Andi decided to look up some sites on miniature dachshunds. She found a picture of some dachshund puppies and attached it to her e-mail, even though they weren't as gorgeous as Tooey's babies. She was about to close the website when a picture of a black-and-tan dachshund with a long silky coat caught her eye.

"Hey, this dog looks familiar!" she said out loud.

At the sound of her voice, Buddy jumped up and planted his paws on her knee. Andi rubbed his ears while she peered at the photo more closely. "Maybe they're related to Tooey or Snowy," she guessed. "I'll ask the Carters. I bet they recognize all their puppies, even when they're grown up." She printed the photo to show them later.

As she lay in bed, trying to go to sleep, Andi took her mind off Cinnamon by thinking about Koko instead. She hoped she'd get to visit him again soon. She pictured the way the little pup had rolled over on her lap so she could rub his tummy. That patch of keyhole-shaped black fur was so unusual, and she loved the way he held her thumb with his tiny paws. He was adorable!

"But not as adorable as you, Bud," Andi said loyally, reaching down to the end of the bed to stroke his silky ears.

The next morning, Tristan, Andi, and Natalie met up on the school steps.

"Cold or what?" Tristan shivered and turned up the collar of his jacket. "I hope Cinnamon managed to keep warm last night. I spoke to Christine after you called me, Nat, and she said he should be fine as long as he doesn't get too cold."

"A catching bucket with plenty of wood chippings in it should be warm enough for him," Natalie said, crossing her fingers for luck.

The bell rang and they made a dash for the door. "I hope Ms. Ashworthy doesn't catch you, Tris," Andi said as they hurried along the corridor. Tristan's strict homeroom teacher wouldn't be pleased to find him going the wrong way at the start of the school day.

Tristan shrugged. "What's a couple of recess detentions to a famous Pet Finder?" All the same, he glanced over his shoulder to be sure Ms. Ashworthy wasn't behind him.

When they reached the classroom, they saw the catching bucket standing in the middle of the room, just as they'd left it.

Andi reached the bucket and peered in. . . .

It was empty!

"Cinnamon's not in the bucket," Andi said heavily.

She heard a startled cry and turned around to see Larissa spin around in the doorway and run down the corridor.

Andi darted after her, but there were so many people streaming toward their classrooms that she was already out of sight. Andi went back into class, determined to ask Larissa some questions the next time she saw her. A few people were peering under the cupboards around the wall. Others were sitting at their desks, talking in subdued voices.

"I'd better go," Tristan said. "Let's meet up later to work out our Plan B." He ran out of the room, nearly colliding with Mr. Dixon.

"Careful, Tristan," he warned.

"Sorry, sir!" He rushed away down the corridor.

"Where's Howard?" Kelly asked as she sat down beside Andi.

"He's going to be a wreck when he hears Cinnamon's missing," said Chen.

"I know," Andi agreed. "I'll give him a call." She took out her cell phone and looked up his number. "Howard, is that you?" she said, when a rather muffled voice answered.

"Yes."

"This is Andi. Are you okay?"

"No. My teeth hurt."

"Listen, I have some bad news. Cinnamon disappeared. He got out of his cage yesterday."

"No way!"

"Andi, put your phone away!" Mr. Dixon called. "I'm about to take attendance."

"Sorry, Howard, I've got to go. See you." Andi hung up.

Larissa came in. Her eyes were red-rimmed from crying, and she deliberately avoided looking at the empty hamster cage as she hurried across the classroom and sat down.

"Are you okay?" Andi whispered.

Larissa fished a tissue out of her pocket and blew her nose. "I . . . I guess." The rest of Andi's questions would have to wait until later.

The class sat quietly while all their names were

called. Looking around the room, Andi saw the same worried expression on every face. Where was Cinnamon? And how were they ever going to find him? He was the smallest pet they'd ever had to search for, and if he wasn't in the classroom, he could be anywhere in the school — or outside it.

At recess, Andi looked around for Larissa. She was peeling a banana at the edge of the schoolyard. As Andi headed over, Natalie ran up and whispered fiercely in her ear.

"I'm sure Larissa knows something about Cinnamon's disappearance. In detective shows, the person who finds the body is usually the prime suspect, and Larissa was there when you noticed Cinnamon had gone!"

"Oh, don't be silly! There hasn't been a crime!" Andi said. Natalie and Larissa weren't great friends, but it sounded like Nat was accusing her of letting Cinnamon out on purpose.

Tristan was playing soccer in the middle of the playground. He stopped when he saw the girls and jogged over. "What's up?"

Natalie told him she was suspicious of Larissa's behavior since Cinnamon's disappearance. Tristan nodded thoughtfully. "She might have stolen him," he suggested.

"Larissa doesn't even like hamsters!" Andi said. She wanted to ask Larissa why she was so upset about Cinnamon, but she didn't think the poor girl was a thief!

"So she says," Natalie said. "But that could be her cover story. Maybe she loves them but pretended to be scared of Cinnamon so no one would suspect her when she stole him."

"Larissa would not steal the class hamster!"

"Then why does she keep crying?" Natalie pointed out. "Looks like a guilty conscience to me."

"Maybe she realizes she shouldn't have done it, but it's too late to do anything about it," Tristan suggested.

Andi couldn't deny that Larissa's reaction was odd. "I think she could know more than she's letting on," she admitted. "That's why I'm going to talk to her."

"I'm coming with you," Tristan said.

"And me!" Natalie said.

Andi raised her eyebrows. "Do you really think that's a good idea, Nat?"

"This is a missing pet investigation," Natalie reminded her. "In case you've forgotten, I'm a member of the Pet Finders Club, too."

Andi knew there was no point arguing. "Okay, but don't start shining a flashlight in her eyes or anything."

They ran over to Larissa just as she finished the last mouthful of her banana.

"We want to talk to you about Cinnamon," Tristan began.

"When exactly did you last see him?" Natalie demanded.

Larissa shrugged helplessly. "I . . . um . . ."

"You were supposed to be taking care of him on the day he vanished," Natalie reminded her.

Andi gave Natalie a hard stare. Grilling Larissa like she was *America's Most Wanted* wouldn't help them find out what had happened! "You must feel really bad about Cinnamon disappearing when you were in charge, Larissa," she said sympathetically. "But you're acting like the whole thing is your fault."

To her dismay, Larissa started crying again. "I'm so sorry! I didn't mean for Cinnamon to run away," she sobbed. "But it *was* my fault. And now we'll never find him again!"

Andi put her arm around Larissa. "Did you forget to close the cage door at lunchtime?"

Larissa cried harder than ever.

"You can tell me," Andi said. She took a packet of tissues out of her backpack and gave one to Larissa. "Here."

Larissa blew her nose. "I d . . . didn't f . . . feed

Cinnamon at l-lunchtime. I was scared of being b-bitten and I couldn't find Howard anywhere. I j-just went to lunch with everyone else. Cinnamon must have escaped because he was hungry." She covered her face with her hands.

Andi started to laugh but quickly turned the laugh into a cough when Larissa looked up at her in dismay. Andi knew there wasn't anything to laugh at — Cinnamon was still missing, after all. But Larissa really didn't need to blame herself. "Hamsters don't eat separate meals," Andi explained. "He wouldn't have gotten out because he'd finished his breakfast and wanted some lunch."

"They nibble little mouthfuls from their pot of food all through the day," Tristan put in.

"It's what hamsters do in the wild," Natalie said. To Andi's relief, Nat sounded much gentler now. "They forage for food when they're hungry. And Cinnamon always has food in his bowl. He couldn't have been hungry, even if it wasn't as full as usual."

"And he usually stores some food in his cheek pouches, too," Andi said. "That's why he has such a fat face."

Larissa looked up. Her face was wet with tears. "So, it might not have been my fault that he got out?"

"Definitely not!" Andi said firmly. "Cinnamon probably didn't even notice his bowl hadn't been filled." She gave Larissa another tissue.

"Thanks." Larissa wiped her eyes. "I feel a lot better. But we still need to find Cinnamon."

"We do." Andi agreed. But if he'd made it out of the school, the catching bucket wasn't going to help at all.

Right after school, Andi and Natalie headed to the Carters' house. Shaun had called them to ask if they would keep an eye on the puppies while they prepared for a dinner party they were hosting that evening. Andi was happy to help, especially because the puppies had been due to have their first vaccinations today and Andi wanted to check that Koko was okay. As usual, Tristan was helping out at Paws for Thought, so he couldn't come.

Eleanor Carter looked rather flustered when she opened the door to Andi and Natalie. She had one arm hooked in the sleeve of a blue jacket. "Hi, girls. Thanks so much for coming."

Inside, the house smelled deliciously of chocolate. "It's a Black Forest gateau," Eleanor explained when she noticed Andi sniffing. "The guests arrive in thirty minutes. I'm running late. I got held up at Dr. Harvey's clinic. It looked like every puppy in Orchard Park was there today. And Shaun had to work late, so I ended up rushing home to let Zan in to see the pups again."

"Did he make up his mind about Koko?" Andi asked.

"Not yet, but he's still very interested. To be honest, I could have done without him coming today, with dinner to prepare, but he looks like such a great owner that I didn't want to put him off."

Tooey sat up when she saw Andi and Natalie come into the living room.

Andi knelt down and petted her. "Hello, girl."

Koko was lying a little apart from his brother and sisters. He was asleep, but he opened his eyes and tried to sit up when Andi stroked his velvety fur with one finger. She scooped him up and laid him on her lap. "I wonder if I can get him to do that nose-wrinkling thing again," she said, rubbing his velvety tummy. She watched him closely, but he lay still, looking up at her with half-closed eyes.

"Are you still feeling a little sleepy, boy?" Andi murmured.

Natalie picked up Leaf. "You can see why people like cream dachshunds. Leaf's patches are a sort of buttery color, and they really stand out." The puppy nibbled her finger. "She's so cute," Natalie giggled, "but I don't think Jet would be too pleased if he had to share me."

Andi turned Koko over and held out her thumb, hoping he'd grab onto it with his paws again. He sniffed her thumb, but snuggled right back down. "Is he all right, do you think?" she asked. "He seems different today."

Natalie shrugged. "It's probably the effects of his shot. Jet was like that when he had his first vaccinations. He was okay the next day, though."

"Maybe going out of the house to the vet's was a shock," Andi thought, tracing the outline of the black patches on Koko's back. "He didn't know the rest of the world existed until today!" She smoothed the fur on the top of his head then put him back into the basket beside Tooey. "I'll let you sleep, Koko. I guess you're too tired to play today."

Tooey stood up, whining. She climbed out of the basket and trotted over to Andi.

"What's up, girl?" she asked.

"Maybe she's getting tired of having the puppies around all the time," Natalie suggested. "It must be a pain, never having a moment to yourself."

"Don't worry, girl," Andi said, stroking Tooey's nose. "They'll all be sold in a few weeks, and then you can have as much time to yourself as you want."

"Should we practice our freestyling tonight before

dinner?" said Natalie. "We could grab Buddy and you could come back to my house."

"Good idea. Let's go now, or we won't have time to go through all our moves." Andi bent over the basket again. "Bye, Koko. I'll see you again soon." She ruffled his ears, but he gave a tiny wail of complaint. "Sorry, boy." Andi stood up, leaving him to snooze.

Natalie put Leaf back in the basket. As she and Andi headed for the door, Tooey trotted after them.

"You stay in here, girl," Andi said gently pushing her back inside. She closed the door behind her. "We're going to go now, if that's okay," she said to Eleanor, popping her head into the kitchen.

Eleanor Carter smiled. "The time away from the puppies has been a real help, and I'm almost finished up in here." She brushed flour from her hands and followed them to the front door. "Thanks again. We'll see you soon."

Halfway down the path, Andi suddenly remembered the photo of the dachshund that she'd printed off the internet. She'd meant to ask the Carters if it was related to their dogs. Glancing back, she saw that the front door was already closed.

No big deal, she thought. *I'll ask them next time.*

*   *   *

Natalie's mom dropped Andi and Buddy back home just before nine o'clock that night. Their practice had gone so well that Andi had stayed for dinner so they could practice again afterward. The only move Buddy still couldn't get the hang of was the sidestep that they'd learned in their last class. It was an advanced move, but Andi was sure they'd get it right if they tried hard enough. Buddy was supposed to move to the side in a straight line, stepping with his back and front feet at the same time. But no matter how many times Andi showed him, he always moved his front feet first, then his back.

"How did it go?" Andi's mom called from the kitchen as Andi shut the front door.

"Excellent! Buddy's doing really well, except for side-stepping. But some of the dogs who've been going to classes forever can't even do that one yet."

"And Jet?"

"He's getting better, too."

"Want anything before bed?" Mrs. Talbot asked.

"No, thanks." Andi kissed her mom then headed up-stairs. "Night, Mom."

"Night, honey. Sleep well." Buddy trotted after Andi.

When she was ready for bed, Andi snuggled down. Buddy circled, then settled in the crook of her legs with a contented sigh.

Andi shut her eyes, her head still full of the music she and Bud were using for their dance. She pictured Buddy gazing up at her as he moved in time with the beat. She loved him so much, from his cute tan-and-white face right down to his paw with the missing claw. She loved the way he laid across her feet when she was working on the computer, and his habit of nudging her with his nose when he wanted to be petted.

As she drifted into sleep, Andi's thoughts turned to Koko. The way he held her thumb with his tiny paws was so cute — and the way he wrinkled his nose and made his ears flap when he shook his head. It was a shame he'd been so sleepy after his trip to the clinic. Andi decided to have a word with Fisher and find out if that was normal.

In her mind, she saw Koko lying sleepily on her lap, his velvety coat dark against her jeans. She imagined tracing her finger around the keyhole-shaped blotch on his tummy. . . .

Andi sat bolt upright in bed. There hadn't been a keyhole-shaped patch on Koko's tummy today!

That wasn't Koko in Tooey's litter at all! It was a totally different puppy!

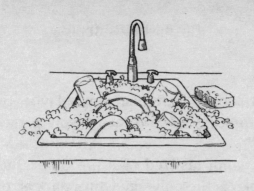

Chapter Seven

Andi leaped out of bed and raced downstairs. "Mom!" she yelled, bursting into the living room. "Something's happened to Koko!" She blurted out everything about going to the Carters' house and about how restless Tooey had seemed. "And Koko was sleepy, and not like his usual friendly self at all. And I've only just realized it's because it wasn't really Koko!" she finished breathlessly.

Her mom looked stunned. "Are you sure, Andi?"

"Yes! He didn't do any of the things he usually did, and the keyhole-shaped patch on his tummy wasn't there. Tooey must have noticed it, too. That was why she was behaving so strangely." Andi ran a hand through her hair.

"Remember when you lost Buddy, Andi?" Mrs. Talbot reminded her. "You followed another Jack Russell terrier that looked just like him. Maybe two of the Carters' puppies look alike and you picked up the wrong one."

"I didn't!" Andi insisted. "All the others have cream patches. Koko is the only one who's dark all over."

Her mom frowned. "Well, the Carters know their own puppies! They'd have noticed if there was something wrong."

"But there *is* something wrong and they *haven't* noticed! Or they hadn't when I was there earlier." Andi could see why her mom didn't believe her — the whole thing sounded impossible — but she knew she was right. Somehow, Koko had been switched!

"If you're really sure, you'll have to tell the Carters tomorrow," her mom said.

"Tomorrow? Oh, Mom, this can't wait!"

"It will have to. It's too late to be calling people now. And it's not like they can do anything about it tonight."

"But, Mom . . ." Andi knew she'd never be able to sleep while she was worrying about Koko.

"No arguments, Andi. Back to bed now. You can speak with Mr. and Mrs. Carter in the morning."

The next morning, Andi met Natalie and Tristan on the corner of the Carters' street. She'd called her friends right after breakfast to tell them about Koko, but they'd all decided it would be better to tell Shaun and Eleanor about Andi's suspicions face-to-face.

Andi had spent most of the night comparing the puppy she'd named with the one she remembered seeing yesterday, and she was more certain than ever that they weren't the same. Having a shot might have made Koko less lively, but no way could it have changed his markings!

But just when she'd convinced herself that she was right about the switch, doubts crowded into her head. She couldn't remember seeing the keyhole-shaped patch on Koko's tummy, but did that mean it definitely wasn't there? Or had she simply not noticed it?

Andi's head ached from turning everything over and over.

"I'm not happy about having to do this," she confessed. "The Carters are going to be so upset."

"You must have it wrong," Tristan said. "How could anyone have switched one of the puppies? The Carters hardly let them out of their sight."

"I know. The whole thing seems impossible."

"If Andi thinks the puppy's not Koko, she's probably right," Natalie defended her.

Tristan shrugged. "I still think we should take a look at the puppy before we say anything."

"Eleanor was rushing around getting ready for a dinner party yesterday," Natalie remembered as they headed along the sidewalk. "She was really stressed about Zan Kirby coming over to look at Koko again." She stopped dead and stared at Andi and Tristan. "Maybe she left Zan alone with the puppies! Maybe *he* switched them!"

Andi was shocked. "But he seemed so nice!"

"Who else could it have been?" Natalie demanded. "And we know he liked Koko. Maybe he couldn't afford to pay for him, so he decided to steal him instead."

Andi frowned. "But where did the other puppy come from?"

"That's what we'll have to find out," Natalie said. "Come on!"

They reached the Carters' house and Tristan rang the doorbell. Andi was so nervous, she felt like a tangle of worms was squirming in her stomach.

Shaun came to the door. He was wearing a pair of rubber gloves and carrying a vase that was dripping soap suds on the carpet. "Hi," he said. "You're out early."

"Who is it, honey?" Eleanor called from the kitchen.

"It's Tooey's biggest fans!" joked Shaun. He opened the door wider. "Come on in."

Andi felt herself blushing as she stepped inside. What if she was wrong? The Carters were nice people and she didn't want to upset them for nothing.

Eleanor came out of the kitchen wearing a plastic apron. "I wasn't expecting to see you back so soon!" she said.

"I . . . um . . ." Andi stammered.

"Is something wrong with Buddy?" Shaun asked, concerned.

Andi shook her head. "No. Buddy's fine. It's . . . it's one of the puppies. Koko. I only thought of it late last night."

"Thought of what?" Eleanor prompted.

"I don't think he *is* Koko."

"What on earth do you mean?" Eleanor gave a gasp.

"He's different," Andi rushed on. "The keyhole patch on his tummy is missing. And yesterday, he didn't do any of the things he usually does, like wrinkling his nose or flapping his ears or holding my thumb. He didn't even wag his tail." She looked desperately at Shaun and Eleanor. "I think he's been switched!"

Shaun darted into the living room. Eleanor followed him, snatching a photo of the puppies from the mantel as she passed. Andi, Tristan, and Natalie ran after her.

They all knelt around the dog basket. Shaun picked up the little chocolate-and-black puppy. "He looks like Koko to me," he said.

"But he's not behaving like Koko," Andi pointed out. The puppy was lying still in Shaun's hands. "Koko would be squirming around and wagging his tail." Andi held out her thumb, but the puppy didn't make a grab for it. "Koko likes holding onto thumbs with his paws."

"Maybe he's still feeling a little woozy from his shot," Shaun suggested.

"Injections don't change the way puppies look," Andi persisted. She ran her fingers over the black patches on his back. Now that she looked closely, she could see *they* were different from Koko's, as well. "These patches are smaller than they should be. And look here." She took the puppy from Shaun and gently turned him over. "Koko has a keyhole-shaped patch on his tummy. But this puppy doesn't."

Eleanor held the photo next to the puppy. The picture showed Koko's tummy clearly.

There was a moment of tense silence, then Shaun said in a shocked voice, "You're right. This puppy's definitely *not* Koko."

"This puppy has a black stripe on his chest and Koko's chest is chocolate brown," Tristan observed.

"And the tip of this pup's ear is brown, while Koko's ears are all black."

Andi didn't know whether to be relieved or horrified. She was glad they'd discovered that the switch had been made, but she couldn't bear to think of poor Koko being separated from his mom, his brother, and his sisters.

Shaun sat back on his heels, bewildered. "I don't understand. How could this have happened?"

"And why?" said Eleanor. "Why would someone steal a puppy and leave another one in its place? It doesn't make any sense."

"Zan Kirby came here yesterday, didn't he?" said Tristan.

"Yes."

"Was he alone with the puppies at any time?" Andi asked.

"For a little while," Eleanor said. "Tooey seemed comfortable with him, and I was in such a rush to get ready for my dinner party. . . ."

"Do you remember anything odd about the way he looked or acted?" Tristan prompted. "Did he bring anything with him, for example?"

"Only a backpack. He said he was on his way to the gym."

"Was the backpack big enough to hold a puppy?" Andi forced herself to ask. Koko would have been so frightened all alone in a stuffy gym bag!

The color drained from Eleanor's face. "I guess it was."

"How long was he with the puppies?" Natalie said.

"About five minutes."

"Long enough to do a switch, then," Tristan said grimly.

"He must have had this puppy in his bag when he arrived," Natalie said.

"There's something else, as well." Eleanor sank down on the arm of the sofa. "Not long after I'd left Zan with Tooey, I found him in the dining room at the back of the house. He said he was looking for the bathroom."

"Or a way out," Andi said grimly. "Maybe he thought Koko would bark and give him away if he didn't get out quickly."

Tristan began to pace up and down. "The thing we've got to figure out is *why* Zan swapped the puppies. He obviously already had a dachshund, so why would he bother to swap it for another one?"

"Maybe he liked Koko better," Andi guessed. "Koko's livelier than this puppy. And he's funnier, too, with all those cute little habits."

"Livelier," Natalie echoed. "Maybe that's it. Maybe

there's something wrong with this puppy, so he swapped it for your healthy one!"

Andi stared at her in dismay. However much she loved Koko, she didn't want there to be anything wrong with the substitute puppy!

They all waited anxiously while Shaun examined the puppy. It lay quietly in his lap while he checked its eyes, ears, teeth, and fur. "I can't see anything obviously wrong with him," he said.

It was some consolation, but Andi was desperately worried about poor Koko. He could be anywhere if Zan had carried him off in his backpack.

"What are we going to do?" Eleanor said. "This is the weirdest crime ever. I'm glad we've got the photos for proof."

"Can *we* look for Koko?" Natalie asked.

"Well, you can try!" said Shaun. "I've heard you Pet Finders are pretty successful. But we should still call the police."

"We could make posters," Andi began, then she shook her head. "There's no point. We already know tiny black-and-brown dachshund puppies look pretty much the same."

"We should go check out Zan Kirby," Tristan said. "Do you have an address or phone number for him?"

Shaun frowned. "We've only corresponded with him by e-mail."

"Well, that's a start," Andi said.

"Come into the study." Eleanor Carter jumped up. "The computer's in there."

The Pet Finders followed her into the cozy room. Eleanor switched on the computer and brought up Zan's e-mails. "Here's his first message."

Dear Mr. and Mrs. Carter,
I'm interested in buying a miniature dachshund puppy. I have owned dachshunds before (see attached photos). I have visited your website many times and would be delighted to own one of your gorgeous puppies. Would it be possible to come and see the most recent litter, please?
Yours sincerely,
Zan Kirby

Eleanor had shown the Pet Finders the photos before, of a gorgeous dachshund with long black-and-tan fur and a smooth-coated fawn dachshund.

"The black-and-tan one looks really familiar," Andi said, frowning at the screen. She thought for a moment, and then let out a gasp. "Of course!" She fished in her

backpack and pulled out the photo she'd downloaded from the Internet. "Look!"

"It's the same dog!" Natalie exclaimed.

"Where did you get that?" Shaun asked.

"I downloaded it from a website."

Natalie looked confused. "Zan Kirby has a website, too?"

Andi shook her head. "I don't think so." She looked at the site details on the bottom of her printout. "There's nothing here about Kirby."

"Let's go to the website," Tristan suggested. "We need to find out if Zan really owned this dog."

The Pet Finders waited impatiently while Eleanor typed in the address, and a colorful page, dotted with photos of miniature dachshunds, appeared on the screen.

"This is Emily Carr's website!" Shaun declared. "She's a top breeder!"

Eleanor pointed to a stunning image of a black-and-tan dog that took pride of place on the home page. The dog was the same as the one in Zan's picture. "There's no way Zan ever owned that dog," she said. "It's one of Emily's main breeding dogs."

"Zan must have downloaded the photo from the Internet to send to you. Which means he lied about owning dachshunds before," Natalie said. "*He must* have switched the puppies." She looked at Andi, her face pale with worry. "I hope we can find him before he does anything to Koko."

"I don't think Zan will hurt him," Andi protested. But of course, there was no way of knowing what he planned to do with the tiny puppy.

Eleanor clicked back to Zan's e-mail, but it didn't contain his home address or his phone number.

"Can't we trace his personal details from his e-mail?" Andi asked.

"It's a really complicated process," Tristan replied gloomily. "You have to have access to Internet service provider records. And I can't see any chance of us getting that."

"Well, we could send him an e-mail asking him to get in touch," Andi persisted. Eleanor clicked the reply button and typed: *Please contact us. Urgent. Shaun and Eleanor Carter.* She included their phone number.

"I don't think he'd reply," Tristan warned darkly. "He won't want any more contact with the Carters after what he's done."

Natalie sighed. "Good point. Right now, it looks like Zan — and Koko — have vanished into thin air."

Chapter Eight

"I'm calling the police," announced Shaun Carter. Grim-faced, he dialed the number and switched on the speakerphone so everyone could hear.

A man answered the phone. "Sergeant Gray speaking. Can I help you?"

"I want to report a stolen puppy," Shaun told him.

"Yes, sir. Can you give me some details?"

The policeman listened while Shaun explained what had happened. When he'd finished, there was an awkward pause. "You don't think you could be mistaken, do you, sir? I mean, one puppy does look very much like another."

"I know my own dogs, Sergeant," Shaun replied. "And I'm telling you that the puppies have been switched. I'm pretty sure I know who did it, too. A man named Zan Kirby."

"I see. And why do you think this Zan Kirby would swap the puppies?"

"I don't know. But he was here yesterday and he had a bag with him big enough to hold a puppy."

The policeman took a deep breath. "Well, perhaps you'd like to take another look at the puppy and make sure it definitely isn't the one you think you've lost. To be honest, your lost puppy falls in the work of the 'missing animals' unit so it isn't really a criminal matter."

"It is if he's been stolen," Shaun protested.

"But you still have the same number of puppies that you started out with," the policeman pointed out. "That sounds like a pretty unusual thief to me. Look, sir, I don't mean to be unsympathetic, but you have to admit this sounds very strange. Perhaps it would be best if you come down to the station to talk about it."

"I'll do that," said Shaun. He said good-bye and hung up.

"That was rude!" Tristan burst out. "Like you can't recognize your own puppy!"

Andi went back to the puppies' basket and crouched beside it. "I wonder where you came from," she said, stroking the impostor's velvety head.

Tooey watched Andi with her head on one side. She had known all along the puppy wasn't hers. Andi rubbed her silky chest. "You're a good girl, Tooey. We need you to look after this poor little guy until we bring Koko home."

"Let's go check the bucket!" Natalie yelled as soon as the bell rang for the start of school on Monday morning. She raced for the door with Tristan close behind her, but Andi got there first. She crossed her fingers for luck as she dashed down the hall, hoping Cinnamon might have turned up.

To her disappointment, the catching bucket was still empty.

"Yet another impossible case for the Pet Finders," Natalie sighed.

"Maybe we should organize a search of the whole school," Andi suggested. "Should I talk to Mr. Dixon about it?"

"Good idea," Tristan agreed.

The rest of the class came crowding in and news of Cinnamon's continued disappearance began to spread.

"I'd better scoot," said Tristan. "Or Ms. Ashworthy'll be on the warpath." He darted out of the room.

"I'll call Howard and give him an update," Andi said, noticing that he still wasn't back at school. "His teeth must be really bad. What on Earth did he have done to them?"

As she took out her cell phone, Natalie grabbed her arm. "Wait! What if there isn't anything wrong with his teeth at all? What if Howard took Cinnamon home with him, and that's why he's staying away from school?"

Andi froze in the middle of calling Howard's number. "Howard wouldn't do a thing like that, Nat."

"Listen. Cinnamon disappeared last Thursday, right?" Natalie ticked off each point on her fingers. "Which was the day Howard left early for his dentist appointment. Remember the way he went on about people not holding Cinnamon right? Maybe he decided Cinnamon shouldn't live at school anymore. We don't know for sure that he even went to the dentist. That might have been an excuse." Natalie flipped her blond hair back from her face. "If you ask me, he's staying home because he doesn't want anyone to figure out he stole Cinnamon!"

Reluctantly, Andi realized Nat had a point. Howard had the opportunity *and* the motive for stealing Cinnamon. But Howard was kind-hearted and funny, and he'd never do anything to upset his friends. Would he? "I guess he might have taken Cinnamon on an impulse," she admitted. "But I'm still going to call him. We need to talk to him."

She called his number.

Just as Howard's phone began to ring, Andi heard someone call her name: "Hey, Andi!"

She spun around. Howard was right there — standing in the classroom doorway. Andi quickly switched off her phone. "Howard! Thank goodness you're here!"

Howard looked at her in surprise. "Why? I've only been gone a day and a half." His right cheek was red and swollen, so he'd obviously been telling the truth about having dental work done.

Andi and Natalie exchanged awkward glances. The evidence against Howard was starting to unravel. "I was worried about you, that's all," Andi said. "You sounded pretty bad when I called on Friday."

"Is there any news? Did you find Cinnamon?" Howard winced and pressed a hand to his cheek. "Ow. Still hurts to talk."

"No, Cinnamon's not back yet," Andi told him. She watched his reaction closely, hating the fact she had to suspect one of her friends of being a hamster thief.

Howard turned pale. "We should organize a search of the whole school," he said determinedly. "He has to be somewhere. Come on, Andi. Let's talk to Mr. Dixon about it."

Natalie opened her mouth to speak, but Andi shot her a look, warning her to keep quiet. Howard's dismay seemed totally genuine. He deserved an award if he was acting. She was even more certain of his innocence when he sadly took a bag of sliced carrots from his backpack and put it beside the empty cage.

"I wanted to give Cinnamon a treat to say welcome back," he sighed.

Andi took his arm. "Come on, let's go talk to Mr. Dixon." She knew Howard would feel better if he was doing something to help find the missing hamster.

"It's a good idea," Mr. Dixon said when Andi and Howard had finished explaining their search plan. "Howard, you pop next door and ask Mrs. Styles if her class can help. Is there anything in particular they should be looking out for, Andi? You're a Pet Finder. I guess you know this sort of thing."

"Cinnamon would probably leave some nibbled paper around," Andi said. "And there might be a few gnaw marks on wooden furniture. And droppings, too."

"Right. Off you go then, Howard. You stay here, Andi, in case there are signs that Cinnamon's been in any of the classrooms. We'll need you and Natalie to go in there and try to follow his trail."

Mr. Dixon sent students to each of the classes to ask their teachers to organize a search. Andi and Natalie waited anxiously, hoping for good news. Even a tiny tooth mark in a sheet of paper might give them the lead they so desperately needed.

One by one, the people Mr. Dixon had sent to organize the searches came back. They all looked disappointed. Cinnamon was nowhere to be found.

"That's that, then," Andi said miserably when Howard, the last to return, appeared in the doorway.

"Cinnamon's nowhere."

Andi sighed. It looked like her worst fear had come true: Cinnamon must have gotten outside!

After school, Andi ran home to fetch Buddy for their Musical Freestyling class while Natalie and Tristan went to pick up Jet. They met up again outside the ASPCA center. The parking lot was full and the lights were on in the windows. Natalie glanced at her watch and sighed. "I've missed most of the obedience class."

"At least we're in time for Freestyling," Andi said.

Fisher's obedience class was just ending when they entered the hall.

Andi, Natalie, and Tristan sat down to wait for the next class to begin. Natalie picked up an animal magazine and began to flip through it, stopping at an article about animal rights.

Andi ruffled Buddy's ears and peered over Natalie's shoulder. "Whoa!" she exclaimed. "This article is written by Alexander Kirby!"

Tristan raised his eyebrows. "So?" Then he sat up straighter. "Oh, do you think he could be related to the Kirby guy who took Koko?"

"No! I think he might be the *same* guy! Think about it. Zan could be short for Ale*xan*der!"

"Wow! You could be right," Natalie said.

"And if he's an *animal* journalist," Andi continued excitedly, "then it's pretty likely he'd be able to get his hands on another puppy to make the switch."

"Andi, you're a genius!" Tristan declared.

Buddy and Jet picked up on the excitement and began to bark. "Shush, Buddy!" Andi said. She glanced around the hall, looking for Shaun Carter — she couldn't wait to tell him about the article! But he and Whisper hadn't arrived yet.

"Let's write down the name of this magazine," Natalie said.

Tristan fished his red notebook out of his backpack

and wrote down the title — *Animal Matters* — along with the company's address and phone number. "We should give them a call tomorrow and ask to speak to Zan. He's got a lot of explaining to do."

Chloe arrived and the class began, though Shaun still hadn't shown up. Andi found it really hard to concentrate. Twice she nearly stepped on Buddy's toes because she kept looking over at the door, hoping to see Shaun coming in.

"Is something wrong, Andi?" Chloe asked.

"I was just wondering where Shaun Carter is. I wanted to talk to him."

"Oh, he's not coming this evening. Eleanor called me earlier to say he had to work late."

"Oh, okay." Andi felt a stab of disappointment, then reminded herself that the Pet Finders couldn't do anything to track down the journalist tonight.

"Sorry, Bud." She rubbed the top of Buddy's head. "I promise I'll watch what I'm doing from now on."

Buddy pricked up his ears as though he were listening to the music. Andi raised her hand and they began to back across the hall.

At lunchtime the next day, the Pet Finders met up in the school yard to call *Animal Matters*. Tristan recited the number without looking it up in his notebook.

"I wish I had a memory like yours," Natalie sighed.

Tristan grinned. "Some of us have it, some of us don't!"

Natalie dialed the number. "I'll use the speakerphone, then we can all hear what Alexander 'Zan' Kirby has to say for himself."

The phone was answered almost at once. "*Animal Matters*," said a woman's voice.

"Hi, there! Can I speak to Alexander Kirby, please?" said Natalie. "I read what he wrote about animal rights, and I've got a great idea for a follow-up article."

"I'm afraid Mr. Kirby is out of the office for an all-day author event, but if you'd like to leave a message, I'll pass it on to him tomorrow."

Natalie left her cell phone number then switched off the phone. "I hope he calls."

"An author event in Orchard Park?" Tristan wondered aloud.

Andi gave a sly smile. "I bet we can go and talk to Zan Kirby in person! He's going to be at Reeder's bookstore."

Tristan looked doubtful. "How do you know?"

"Andi's psychic," Natalie said in a spooky voice.

"Don't forget she was the one who sensed that Koko had been switched."

"No, we saw posters about a book signing in Reeder's window," Andi explained. "Remember, Nat? Dale Savage is coming to promote his new book. And it's exactly the sort of thing that would appeal to *Animal Matters* readers. Besides, how many famous authors could there be in Orchard Park on the same day?" She pulled out her phone again. "I'll call Shaun and Eleanor to tell them that we've tracked down Zan and that we're hoping to speak to him this afternoon."

"Yep," said Tristan, "he's going to have some *very* tricky questions to answer!"

Chapter Nine

The Pet Finders dashed out of school the moment the bell rang at the end of the day. Andi couldn't wait to get to the bookstore. They had to be getting close to finding Koko now!

As they headed for the sidewalk, Tanya McLennan brushed past in a hurry and didn't bother to say good-bye.

"The animal cage!" Tristan exclaimed, stopping dead in the middle of the sidewalk.

Andi and Natalie stared at him. "The animal cage?" Andi asked.

"Tanya got a cage. Don't you remember? We delivered it for Mike."

Andi frowned. "So? It was for a mouse."

"She *said* it was for a mouse," Tristan agreed. "But what if it was for a hamster? One hamster in particular. . . ."

Andi's head spun. Were they going to end up suspecting everyone in their class of stealing Cinnamon?

"Let's get her!" Natalie shot off along the sidewalk, where Tanya was just opening a car door.

"Wait, Tanya!" Andi yelled, sprinting past Natalie.

Tanya glanced around, startled. "Oh, hi, Andi."

"That hamster cage we delivered," Andi panted, skidding to a halt beside Tanya.

"What about it?"

Andi thought fast. She could hardly accuse Tanya of stealing Cinnamon just because she'd had a hamster cage delivered. "I . . . I was just wondering whether you could bring your mouse to school, maybe. The smell of another small rodent might attract Cinnamon back to the classroom."

"Sorry, I still don't have the mouse yet." Tanya opened the car door and climbed inside. "Sorry I can't help," she called through the window as her mom drove away.

"This is starting to look pretty suspicious," said Andi.

Natalie nodded. "I think we need to talk to Tanya again — fast!"

"What about the book signing?" Tristan said. "We don't want to miss Zan."

"It doesn't start until four o'clock," Andi said, remembering the poster in the bookstore window. "There's just enough time to talk to Tanya first." She set off running.

"Whoa!" Tristan called after her.

Andi skidded to a halt and looked back impatiently. "What? We can't waste any time!"

"Let's take the bus!" Tristan said. He and Natalie darted across the road to where a bus was just pulling up.

Andi raced back and jumped onto the bus as well.

They all sat down on the long back seat.

"It wouldn't have taken long to run to Tanya's house," Andi pointed out. "It's probably only a couple of stops. And I've been so busy with freestyling and puppies that I haven't been running for forever."

"No, thanks," said Tristan.

"Agreed," Natalie added. She took out a compact mirror and checked her reflection. "Besides, running messes up my hair." She pushed a strand of hair behind her ear and put the mirror away again.

"Right, Nat. You can't possibly let Tanya see you with messed-up hair," Andi teased.

"Should I be going for your look?" Natalie asked innocently.

Andi caught sight of her own reflection in the bus window and broke off. Her own hair was sticking up all over! "You could have told me!" she protested.

"If you two could stop discussing your hair for two seconds," Tristan cut in, "you'd notice we need to get off here."

The bus stopped at the end of Tanya's street. Her mom's car was parked in the driveway. "Good, they're home already," said Andi.

"What are we going to say to her?" Tristan asked as he rang the bell.

"Maybe you could tell her Christine has some mice for sale, Tris," Andi suggested.

"Or we could just ask her straight out if she knows anything about Cinnamon's disappearance," said Natalie.

Suddenly, the door opened, and Tanya's little sister Marie appeared on the step. "Hello," she said.

Andi stared at her in astonishment. Marie was holding Cinnamon!

"Look at my hamster!" said Marie, holding up Cinnamon proudly. "He's for my birthday!"

Andi was speechless. Tanya had stolen Cinnamon for her sister's birthday present!

"He's beautiful," Tristan said in a strained voice. "Is Tanya here?"

Tanya came out of a door in the hallway. She turned bright red when she saw the Pet Finders. "You'd better come in," she mumbled. "Marie, you should go and put your hamster in his cage."

Andi, Natalie, and Tristan followed Tanya upstairs to her bedroom. Andi could hardly believe what was happening. One of their classmates was a thief after all!

"How could you, Tanya?" Natalie burst out as soon as the bedroom door was closed. "You stole Cinnamon!"

Tanya hung her head. "I know it was wrong, but I wanted to get Marie a really memorable birthday present. She's been so sick! I thought she deserved something special."

"Oh, yeah! A stolen hamster is really memorable!" Natalie said.

"You could have *bought* a hamster at Paws for Thought," Tristan pointed out.

"I know. And I *did* look for hamsters in the store, but Marie's favorite color is orange and the pet store didn't have any hamsters that color. I knew Cinnamon would be perfect."

"Our whole class has been worried sick!" Andi said. "Didn't you care?" She could see that Tanya was upset, but she deserved to feel bad after what she'd done.

"I thought we'd just get a new hamster to replace

him," Tanya said in a quavery voice. Her eyes filled with tears. "It was awful when I saw how upset everyone was, but it was too late to admit it by then. You'd all have been mad at me."

"We *are* mad at you!" Natalie snapped. "Cinnamon doesn't belong to you!"

"I know! I wish I could turn everything back to how it was, but I can't." Tanya threw herself down on the bed and buried her face in her pillow. "I only did it for Marie!"

"What are we going to do?" Andi whispered to Tristan and Natalie. "Tanya's going to be in monster trouble at school when this gets out."

"Good!" Natalie said.

"I know it was wrong," Tanya sobbed, sitting up. "And I promise I'll never do anything like this again. Ever!"

"We should help her, Nat," Andi said. "She seems to have learned her lesson."

Natalie looked shocked. "If you've got a plan to sort things out, I'm listening."

"Me, too," said Tristan.

"What's going to happen now?" Tanya asked tearfully.

Andi sat beside her on the bed. "First, you have to tell your mom where Cinnamon really came from."

Tanya gulped. "I'll be grounded for a year!"

"If you don't tell her, we will," Natalie warned. "And it would sound better coming from you."

"But *we'll* tell Marie, if you want," Andi offered. She knew Tanya was going to find it hard enough confessing the truth to her mom.

Tanya nodded. "Thanks." She stood up and dried her eyes. "I'll go get Marie; then I'll talk to my mom."

A few moments later, Marie came in looking puzzled. "What?"

"We've got some bad news, Marie," Tristan said gently.

Marie's eyes widened. She picked at a HAPPY BIRTHDAY! 5 TODAY! badge pinned to her sweatshirt and Andi realized it was actually her birthday *that* day. That made everything a hundred times worse!

"When Tanya gave you Cinnamon, she wanted you to have a really special present," Andi began. "The problem is, Cinnamon already belonged to somebody else."

Marie's bottom lip quivered. "Who?"

"Cinnamon belongs to lots of people," Andi said. "And they all miss him very much."

Marie gasped. "They want him back?"

"Yes, they do," Andi replied. "They didn't want Tanya to take Cinnamon in the first place." She glanced at the others, hoping they agreed with her decision to avoid talking about the theft. Natalie gave her an encouraging nod.

"So, it was a boo-boo?" Marie asked.

"That's right," said Andi. "Cinnamon can't be your pet because he still belongs to these other people."

"But — you can choose a *new* hamster from the pet store," said Tristan, "and it will be just as cute as Cinnamon!"

Marie gazed at them in dismay. "But Cinnamon is *my* hamster. I want to teach him tricks."

"You can teach your *new* hamster tricks," Natalie promised. "And if you choose it yourself, you'll be able to pick the one with the prettiest color!"

Marie nodded hesitantly. "Yeah."

"And Cinnamon belongs to our class, so you can come in and see him whenever you come to get Tanya from school," Andi told her.

Marie looked a little more cheerful. "Okay! Then I'll have two hamsters — one at home and one at school! I'll go and tell him." She went out of the room.

Tristan rubbed his hands over his face. "Glad that's over."

"Me, too," said Natalie.

"Come on," Andi said heavily. "We can't stay up here."

They trooped downstairs. As they reached the bottom, Tanya and Mrs. McLennan came out of the kitchen. Tanya's eyes were red-rimmed and her mom looked angry.

"Tanya's told me all about Cinnamon," said Mrs. McLennan. "I'll tell Marie to bring him down."

"I have a shoebox in my room," Tanya said. "We could put Cinnamon in there." She hurried upstairs to get it.

Mrs. McLennan tried to smile at the Pet Finders. "I'm so sorry Tanya has caused all this trouble."

"Don't worry, Mrs. McLennan," said Tristan. "The main thing is we found Cinnamon safe and sound."

Marie came downstairs, carrying Cinnamon in her hands. "You have to go back home," she whispered, looking tearful.

Tanya appeared behind her with the shoebox. She had made some holes in the lid so that Cinnamon would be able to breathe, and she'd put plenty of shredded paper inside to keep him warm.

Marie gulped. "You'll like it at school, Cinnamon," she said. "I'll come and see you lots, I promise!" She placed him gently in the box, and Tanya put on the lid.

Tristan took out his cell phone. "I'll give Christine Wilson, the owner of Paws for Thought, a call to see if she's got any orange hamsters."

"Can I give Cinnamon a lettuce leaf, Mom?" Tanya asked.

"Sure, honey," said Mrs. McLennan.

Tanya fetched a leaf from the crisper. As she slipped it into the box, Andi heard her whisper, "Sorry, Cinnamon."

"Christine's got a new litter of hamsters, and some of them have tan markings," Tristan announced, switching off his cell phone.

"That's great," Mrs. McLennan said. "Do you hear that, Marie? We can go and choose a new hamster right away."

Marie smiled.

"We should go," Andi said. She picked up the box and carried it carefully out of the house. Natalie and Tristan followed her.

As they walked down the driveway, Tanya ran after them. "Wait! What about school? Are you going to tell everyone what I did?"

Andi looked at Tristan and Natalie.

Tristan shrugged. "I guess the important thing is that Cinnamon will be back where he belongs."

"Nat?" Andi prompted.

Natalie looked thoughtful. "I guess we could put Cinnamon in the catching bucket early in the morning, so it will look like he made his own way back."

Andi nodded. "That sounds like a good idea."

"Thank you so much! I promise I'll never steal anything again!" Tanya crossed her heart.

Looking at her pale, anxious face, Andi really believed her.

Chapter Ten

There was no time to take Cinnamon home, so Andi tucked the box inside her jacket to shield the little hamster from the chilly wind. When they turned onto Main Street, they could see that the bookstore was packed with people listening to Dale Savage read a chapter from his book. He was a suntanned, older man, with collar-length light hair and a handsome face. About fifty people were sitting on chairs and almost as many were standing around the back and sides of the store. Andi, Natalie, and Tristan squeezed into a tiny gap just inside the door.

"Can you see him?" Andi asked, stretching up on tiptoe and craning her neck to see past the people in front of her.

"Over there," a lady said kindly, pointing to Dale

Savage. "I'm surprised you don't recognize him from TV."

"Oh, yeah, thanks," Andi said, trying not to giggle. She wasn't looking for Dale Savage.

"Look, there!" Natalie said in a low voice, pointing across the room. Right at the back, standing on a chair and taking notes, was a familiar red-haired figure, Zan Kirby.

"Come on!" Tristan whispered. He began to push through the crowd, trying to reach the journalist.

"Excuse me!" a man hissed. "These seats are taken. You'll have to stand."

"I don't want to sit down," Tristan whispered, going red. "I want to speak to someone over there."

"You'll have to wait until there's more space!" the man told him.

"Come back, Tris," Andi said, pulling him away. "If we stay near the door, Zan can't leave until we've talked to him."

Dale Savage was still reading: "The most important thing is that dogs recognize you as pack leader. If your dog is lying on the chair you want to sit on, make him get up and move. It might seem mean, but your dog will love you for it in the end because he'll understand that he's part of your pack, not the other way around." He closed his book. "Does anyone have any questions?"

Tristan's hand shot up.

"Yes, over there," said Dale.

"Come through to the front so Dale can see you," said a lady wearing a store name tag.

"I hope he's not going to do anything stupid," Natalie said to Andi, as Tristan wriggled to the front of the crowd.

Tristan stood beside Dale and pointed dramatically at Zan Kirby. "Actually, I want to speak to that journalist over there." Zan looked shocked. "We know what you did to the Carters!"

Everyone turned to stare at Zan. The color drained from his face and he stared at Tristan in dismay.

"I . . . I . . ." He stepped down from his chair, looking startled. "Listen, let's go outside and talk about this," he suggested. "I can explain everything," he told the people around him.

Andi watched Zan push his way toward the door. It was taking him so long, she was afraid he'd have time to think up a believable story before he got to them.

The man who'd reprimanded Tristan blocked Zan's way. "We came here to listen to Dale, not to watch you and this boy solve your personal problems."

"Sorry," Zan said. "I just want to get past. . . ."

The man shifted reluctantly and Zan reached the door. He looked even more startled to see Andi and Natalie waiting for him. He obviously recognized them.

Tristan came over, his hair sticking up on end. "Well?" he demanded.

Zan Kirby shook his head. "I'll tell you everything, but not here where everyone can listen."

"We can talk outside," Andi said. She didn't want to give Zan any more time to think up a good story.

A cold wind was blowing outside and Andi pulled her jacket tighter around the shoebox, remembering what Tristan had said about hamsters needing warmth.

Natalie turned to face Zan as soon as they reached the sidewalk. "You were never going to buy one of the Carters' puppies, were you? You just wanted to switch your puppy with Koko."

"Switch? What do you mean?" Zan looked bewildered.

"Were you planning to buy one of their puppies?" Natalie prompted.

Zan looked uncomfortable. "Well, not exactly."

"I knew it!"

"But I still don't know anything about a switch," Zan insisted. He glanced around, then lowered his voice. "Look, I'm an investigative journalist, and I'm writing an article about puppy farms. I've been pretending to be a prospective buyer so I can investigate breeders."

"But the Carters look after their dogs really well," Andi protested. "You don't have to investigate them!"

Zan nodded impatiently. "I know that now. I visited them twice because they seemed too good to be true, and I wanted to check their total set-up, not just the bits they wanted me to see." He fished in his bag and took out a Dictaphone. "Listen. This will prove it." He switched it on and they heard his voice, speaking quietly: "Mother dog in good health. Eyes and teeth clean. Coat good condition. Fresh water available." He switched it off. "Okay?"

Andi had to admit it looked like he was telling the truth. "So you really don't know anything about the switch?"

"What switch?"

"Koko, the black-and-chocolate puppy that you liked best, has been swapped with a puppy from another litter," she told him.

Zan's eyes lit up and Andi remembered he was a journalist. This was the sort of scoop that his readers would love! "Why would anyone do a thing like that?" he asked.

"We're not sure," Andi admitted.

"We also don't know *how*," said Natalie. "The puppies haven't been alone with anyone except you."

Zan grinned unexpectedly. "In that case, I can see how you thought I was the culprit. Good detective work!"

"We're the Pet Finders Club," Andi explained.

"The Pet Finders Club?" Zan echoed.

"Yep," Tristan said. "We do stuff like this all the time. But this is one of our trickier cases."

Zan took out his notebook. "I think there's a story here. Can I cover it for *Animal Matters*?"

"It's okay with us, but you'd have to ask the Carters," Tristan said. He looked at Andi and Natalie. "And it looks like we're going to have to do a lot more detective work to solve this case."

"Let me know if I can help in any way," said Zan, handing them his card.

"Thanks," Tristan said. He pulled a Pet Finders flyer from his backpack for Zan. "Good luck with your investigation."

"We should tell the Carters that it wasn't Zan who took Koko," Andi said when Zan had gone back into the bookstore. She lifted the lid of the shoebox to check that Cinnamon was all right. He was curled up in the middle of the shredded paper, fast asleep.

"We must be missing something," Natalie sighed as

they set off toward the Carters' house. "The puppies must have been left on their own with someone else."

"Hang on," Andi interrupted, stopping so suddenly that Tristan almost walked into her. "Eleanor took Tooey and the puppies to Dr. Harvey's clinic the day Koko disappeared. She said it looked like every puppy in town was there having shots."

"Maybe the nurse mixed up two litters while she was putting them back in their baskets," Natalie said excitedly.

Andi handed Cinnamon to Tristan and took out her cell phone. "I'll call the Carters and find out if that could have happened. But it's four forty-five. We've got to get over to the clinic."

Eleanor Carter answered the phone.

"Hey, it's Andi. We have news — Zan Kirby definitely didn't switch the puppies."

"How do you know?"

"We've spoken to him. He's a journalist, and he was doing an undercover investigation on puppy farming."

Eleanor gasped.

"It's okay," Andi said quickly. "He really liked your set-up, and he knows you're great breeders. But we just remembered — you took the puppies to the clinic that day. Were you with the puppies the whole time?"

There was a pause from Eleanor before she replied. "I left them at the front desk for a few minutes while I used the restroom. But Dr. Harvey's receptionist is very reliable. She would never have allowed puppies to be switched."

"It could have happened by accident," Andi said. "Maybe there was another litter of dachshunds there, too. We'll go to the clinic right now to find out. Thanks, Eleanor." She hung up quickly.

"Well?" Tristan demanded.

Andi held up her crossed fingers. "Dr. Harvey's clinic, quick!"

Dr. Harvey, a tall man with gray hair and kind eyes, was in the empty waiting room, chatting with his receptionist when the Pet Finders burst in. "What's the emergency?" he joked.

"We're investigating a missing puppy case," Tristan puffed.

"It's Koko, one of the Carters' puppies," Natalie added.

Dr. Harvey frowned. "Koko's missing? Poor Shaun and Eleanor! They must be so worried."

"The thing is," Andi continued, "Koko was switched with another puppy, and we think it might have happened here. By mistake," she added hastily, as the receptionist looked horrified.

"That's impossible!" she said. She was wearing dog-shaped earrings, and a silver cat brooch was pinned to the collar of her blouse, next to a name badge that read Teresa. "Puppies stay in their carriers until they're in the consulting room. The Carters' puppies couldn't possibly have been mixed up with another litter."

"Well, if it didn't happen by accident," Natalie said, "someone must have deliberately switched the puppies."

"But why would anyone do that?" Teresa asked.

"I don't know, but I think I know how they did it!" Tristan declared. "It's like that old story about stealing a wheelbarrow from a construction site. The guard will let you through when he sees the wheelbarrow is empty."

"What are you talking about, Tris?" Natalie said. "We're looking for a puppy, not a wheelbarrow."

"But it's the same thing. Nobody would have thought anything was strange if someone brought in a puppy." Tristan turned to Teresa. "Could you check your records and see if anyone else brought a miniature dachshund in that day?"

"There *was* another miniature dachshund," she

agreed. "I remember him. A sweet little thing." She flipped over a couple of pages in the appointment book. "Here we are. The puppy belonged to someone named Sinden. It was his first visit to the clinic."

"He must have come just to switch puppies!" said Tristan.

"So, we know who might have done it, and how," Andi said. "But we still don't know why."

"We thought there might have been something wrong with the puppy that was left in Koko's place," Natalie told Dr. Harvey. "But Shaun Carter thought he looked okay."

Dr. Harvey frowned. "It's not always apparent. Sometimes puppies suffer from inherited disorders that only show up after tests. For example, *acanthosis nigricans* is a common skin complaint in dachshunds, and that won't show until a pup's about three months old. An eye disorder called *corneal dystrophy* can affect dachshunds, too."

"So the puppy could be sick after all?" Andi asked in dismay.

"Possibly. We need to get him checked out," Dr. Harvey replied. "I'll call Shaun and Eleanor and ask them to bring him in. And it's vital to track down his owner, because he could know exactly what's wrong with him."

"Can we have Mr. Sinden's address?" Natalie asked.

"I'm sorry," Dr. Harvey said. "We can't give out addresses because of patient confidentiality." He looked as if he was about to say something else, but just then a flustered lady rushed in, looking very red in the face and staggering under the weight of a heavy pet carrier.

"I have an emergency!" she declared.

Dr. Harvey and Teresa went to help her, leaving the Pet Finders standing by the counter.

"I think we should go," said Natalie. "We aren't going to get Sinden's address here."

"Maybe he's in the phone book," Andi said. "We could head back to your house, Nat, and look him up."

She and Nat held the door open for Tristan, who walked slowly, holding Cinnamon's box steady.

"It's funny," Andi said once they were outside. "I feel like I've heard the name Sinden before, but I can't think where."

They headed for Natalie's house, weaving their way carefully between last-minute shoppers on the main street so Cinnamon wouldn't be bumped around.

Suddenly, Tristan shouted. "Hey!"

"What?" Andi asked eagerly.

"There's the Banana Beach Café! Why don't we talk about the case there, over a muffin? I'm sure we could borrow their phone book."

"That's it!" Andi cried out.

"*What*'s it?" Natalie asked, puzzled. "Really into muffins all of a sudden?"

"I just remembered where I've heard the name Sinden before. Remember those pastries that were sent to school, just before Cinnamon disappeared? *Lance Sinden* is the new pastry chef at The Treetop Hotel! There can't be *that* many Sindens in Orchard Park!"

Chapter Eleven

Andi called Shaun Carter that night to tell him what they'd learned. "I've never heard of Lance Sinden in dog-breeding circles," he said, "but if he *is* the thief, I don't want you going anywhere near him on your own."

"Natalie's reserved a table for us at the hotel for tea tomorrow," Andi said. "I couldn't get a reservation on my own, but her parents are regulars."

"I'm free tomorrow. Why don't I come with you?" Shaun suggested.

"Perfect!"

"What time?"

"Five o'clock. That gives us time to change after school." Andi paused. "Natalie says we need to look nice or the hotel won't let us in." She hoped Shaun wouldn't be offended, but she'd never seen him wearing anything but faded, dog-friendly jeans and an old sweatshirt.

"Don't worry, I'll dress up for the occasion," Shaun said good-humoredly.

"We'll meet you there, then," Andi said.

The next morning, Natalie brought Cinnamon to school in the shoebox.

"Is he okay?" Andi asked.

Natalie glanced around to make sure no one was watching them, then lifted the lid. Cinnamon looked up at Andi, his beady eyes bright and curious as he nibbled the sunflower seed he held between his front paws.

"He's so cute," Andi sighed. "Everyone will be really happy to have him back."

"We're going to have to sneak him inside before the bell rings," said Tristan. He made a face. "Let's hope Ms. Ashworthy's not on the prowl."

They hurried to the main door, but there were two teachers talking in the entrance hall. "Let's try around the side," Andi suggested.

There was a fire-escape door near the classroom that the janitor sometimes left propped open when he was working outside. Luckily for them, today it was open.

The janitor was unblocking a drain nearby. He was kneeling down with his back to them, pushing a rod into the drain.

"We'll have to be quiet," Natalie whispered.

They crept toward the door. Andi's heart pounded so hard it was a wonder that Nat and Tris couldn't hear it. If they were caught, it would wreck their plan to sneak Cinnamon inside without anyone finding out what had really happened.

Luckily, the janitor was humming to himself and didn't hear them sneak past. Keeping a wary eye out for teachers, they tiptoed along the corridor.

Suddenly they heard footsteps heading their way. "In here, quick!" Tristan whispered, flinging open a door. They squeezed into the cramped cupboard and Tristan pulled the door shut, plunging them into darkness.

"Can you move over a little, Andi?" Natalie hissed. "I've got a broom handle digging into my back!"

"Sorry. I don't have much space, either. My face is squished against a can of furniture polish!" The smell was making Andi's eyes water, and she tried hard not to sneeze.

"Shhh," Tristan warned.

The footsteps passed by outside. "Stay here," Tristan whispered. "I'll see if the coast's clear."

He cautiously opened the door and looked out. "So far, so good."

Andi watched him tiptoe along the hallway. At the corner, he stopped and looked back, then beckoned them forward.

"Come on, Nat." Andi felt an urge to giggle. "It feels like we're in a spy movie!"

They reached the classroom without meeting any teachers, and Natalie lifted the hamster out of the shoebox and placed him safely in the catching bucket. "There!" she said. "Nobody will ever guess he wasn't in the building the whole time."

She was interrupted by the bell ringing.

"Quick!" said Andi. "We don't want anyone to find us in here."

Natalie stuffed the shoebox in her backpack, then they scurried out of the classroom and along the corridor, heading toward the main entrance. As soon as they saw kids hurrying to class, they turned and sauntered back the way they had come, as if they'd been the first into the building.

Andi and Natalie hung their coats in the locker room to give someone else a chance to discover Cinnamon. As Nat had said, the person to find the body was usually the culprit.

By the time they went into the classroom, an excited crowd had gathered around the catching bucket.

"Andi, he's back!" Howard called. "The catching bucket worked!"

Andi, Natalie, and Tristan hurried over. "Awesome!" Andi exclaimed. And she really meant it. She was so glad to have the little hamster back.

Howard lifted Cinnamon out of the bucket and looked him over. "He's obviously been eating okay. He doesn't look thin, or anything." He ran his finger over the hamster's head. "I'm glad you're back, boy."

Cinnamon sat up on Howard's hand, his nose quivering, and cleaned his face with his tiny paws.

"Let's get you back in your cage," Howard said. "Can you open the door for me, Larissa?"

"Sure! And I'll get him some fresh bedding." Larissa touched Cinnamon's head with one finger. The hamster went on washing his face. Larissa stroked him gently, her face breaking into a smile. "His fur's so soft," she said breathlessly. "I don't know why I was scared of him."

Tanya came into class. She stopped in the doorway and looked warily at Andi and Natalie.

"Hey, Tanya!" Howard called. "We got Cinnamon back. The catching bucket worked!"

"Awesome!" said Tanya. As she approached Andi, she whispered, "Thanks!"

"Did Marie choose a new hamster?" Andi asked in a low voice.

"Yeah. A cute little golden one." Tanya smiled. "She wanted to call it Cinnamon, but Mom persuaded her that Spice would be a better name. I think one Cinnamon is enough."

The Pet Finders arrived at the hotel just before five o'clock. Andi was surprised at how luxurious the lobby was. The floor was tiled with pink-veined marble, and huge marble pillars supported the high ceiling. An immaculately dressed woman stood at the reception counter, a classy leather attaché on her shoulder.

"Wow! This place is sooo nice," Andi whispered.

Natalie looked surprised. "Do you think so? My mom and I always have tea here after we've been shopping."

A bellboy in a blue uniform and cap directed them to the dining room. All of the hotel staff were wearing bow ties, and the head waiter addressed Natalie as *Miss Lewis.*

Shaun was waiting for them at their table, wearing a button-down shirt and a tie. A pale linen jacket was slung over the back of his chair. "They let me in," he joked, "so I must look nice enough." Then he became more serious. "I took the impostor puppy to Dr. Harvey today. He'll need to run some tests to check all the possibilities in case his real owner can't be found."

"So that's two dachshunds in danger," Andi said. "Let's hope this lead takes us somewhere."

"And while we're waiting to find out more about Lance Sinden," Tristan said, "we might as well have some food. I'm starving!"

"I've already ordered a selection of finger sandwiches," Shaun said. "Is that all right?"

"Wonderful!" Andi said, smoothing down her wool skirt. "Thank you very much."

"Yes, thank you!" chimed in Tristan and Natalie.

Andi looked around the dining room. It had a high, ornate ceiling, walls covered in rich red wallpaper, and a carpet so soft and thick that the waiters' feet made no noise at all. The high-backed chairs were painted gold, with red padded seats, the tables were covered with crisp white cloths, and the china was edged in finely etched flowers.

"This must be what it's like to eat with the Queen of England," Tristan whispered.

A crisply dressed waiter brought a tray of sandwiches to their table. Another brought a pitcher of juice.

Shaun thanked them. "So, what's the plan?" he asked when the waiters were out of earshot.

"We're going to ask if we can speak to the new pastry chef," Tristan explained. "And when Lance Sinden appears, we'll confront him about the puppy switch." He took a sandwich.

A waiter soon came over. "Is everything to your satisfaction?"

"Yes, wonderful, thank you," Natalie said politely.

"The best!" Andi agreed. She took a deep breath. This was their chance! "Could I speak to the new pastry chef? He sent some delicious pastries to my class a little while ago, and I'd like to say thank you in person."

The waiter smiled. "Lance would be really pleased to meet you, Miss, but he only works in the mornings."

"Oh, no!" Tristan exclaimed. "I want to be a pastry chef when I grow up, and I was hoping he could give me some advice."

"Well, you could always pop in and see him one morning," the waiter suggested.

Tristan swallowed the last of his sandwich and stood up. "Thanks very much. I'll do that."

Shaun paid the bill and they left the hotel. "What luck. Maybe we should book a table for morning coffee."

"We'd have to wait 'til Saturday," Andi groaned. "And

poor Koko . . ." She broke off and gripped Natalie's arm. "Look!" She pointed to a pair of wide-legged white trousers and a white jacket that were hanging on a clothesline beside a long, two-story apartment block. "That's the sort of uniform worn by a chef, isn't it?"

"Well, a chef might want to live close to his restaurant — especially a pastry chef." Natalie agreed. "They start work really early in the morning. My mom's friend is married to a pastry chef, and he sometimes starts work at three A.M. I guess I just didn't think about them finishing early, too."

"I wonder if his name would be on his uniform," Tristan said. "Should we go see?"

They hurried along the driveway that ran between the hotel and the apartment block. "You guys are amazing," marveled Shaun. "You never give up!"

As they stopped beside the clothesline, a small blue car came into the parking lot and stopped in front of the apartments. A tall woman wearing a red windbreaker and a red headscarf decorated with dogs climbed out.

"That's Stella Milton!" Shaun exclaimed, dumbfounded. "She breeds miniature dachshunds, too. This is getting weird."

"Is she a friend?" Andi asked.

"Not really a friend," Shaun admitted. "More of a show

rival, really!" He grinned. "Her dogs used to be hot competition for Tooey and Snowy." He raised his voice. "Hello, Stella! This is a surprise."

The woman turned around. "Shaun!" she gasped. "How . . . nice to see you!"

"Did you hear? Tooey's had her pups." Shaun said. "Four girls and — "

Stella Milton didn't let him finish. "Yes, yes! I saw them on your website." She looked around. "Oh, dear, I seem to have come to the wrong place. Excuse me!" She hurried back to her car.

Just then, a young man with curly brown hair looked out of a first-floor window. "Hey, Aunt Stella! Where are you going?"

For a moment, Stella didn't move. Then she slammed her car door again and locked it. She smiled awkwardly at Shaun and the Pet Finders and stalked toward the apartment block.

"I'll come and let you in!" the young man yelled.

"I'm so sorry, Lance," Andi heard Stella Milton say when he arrived at the door. "I thought I was early. I didn't want to disturb . . ." her voice trailed off as she moved farther away.

"She called him Lance!" Tristan whispered excitedly. "That must be Lance Sinden! Lance is a pretty unusual name, so the chances of there being two of them around here must be slim. Come on!"

Andi reached the door of the building first and caught it just before it closed. She poked her head in and saw Stella and the young man go into one of the apartments and shut the door behind them.

"It's that one," Andi said, pointing down the hall when the others caught up. "I wonder if we could hear what they're saying if we got closer."

"Let's think about this first," Tristan said. "If you look at the facts, Lance was at the clinic with a miniature dachshund puppy on the day Koko was switched. . . . "

"And Lance is related to Stella Milton, a breeder who happens to be one of Shaun and Eleanor's biggest rivals," Natalie put in.

"That's a motive, isn't it?" asked Andi.

They crept up to the apartment door and pressed their ears to it.

"I guess you'll want to take the puppy now," Lance Sinden was saying.

"Fast," came the reply. "I've got to get him out of here without Shaun seeing!"

Andi glanced excitedly at Natalie and Tristan. It looked like they'd found Koko!

Chapter Twelve

Andi heard a tiny bark. "That sounds like Koko!" she whispered, and Natalie nodded.

"I wish we could see what they're doing," Tristan said. "Do you think we should knock on the door?"

Before anyone could answer, they heard Stella say: "I'll be off, then." She sounded as though she were on the other side of the front door.

"She's leaving!" Andi hissed, feeling suddenly nervous about confronting the thieves. She, Natalie, and Tristan drew back a little, forming a line to stop Stella Milton from getting past.

The front door opened, and there stood Stella with a wriggling black-and-tan bundle in her arms.

"How could you do something like this, Stella?" Shaun demanded.

"What do you mean? Let me pass!" Stella protested. "I have to take this puppy to the veterinarian."

"I don't think you do!" Shaun lifted Koko out of her hands and handed him to Andi.

Andi tipped the puppy gently onto his back. "There's the keyhole patch!" she exclaimed. "It *is* Koko!" To her relief, he looked clean and well-fed. His little tail wagged furiously against her wrist, and he batted Andi's thumb with his front paws when she turned him over again. Andi bent down and kissed his nose.

Lance Sinden came out of his apartment. "What's going on? Aunt Stella, are you all right?"

"You've stolen one of my puppies, Stella," Shaun said angrily. "And I'm going to report it to the police."

"No!" Stella cried. "Please, Shaun. Don't involve the police!"

Two people came down the hall and stopped to watch what was going on.

Lance Sinden looked stunned. "The police?" he echoed. "Look, I don't know what's going on, but you'd better come inside and sort this out."

He led them into his apartment. The living room was a bright, spacious room furnished with leather arm-chairs and a glass-and-chrome coffee table. Stella sank into a chair, somehow managing to look frightened and indignant at the same time. Lance sat opposite her, and Andi, Natalie, and Koko shared the third armchair. Natalie stroked the puppy's head as he lay in Andi's arms, and he licked her fingers with a tiny pink tongue. Tristan sat on the floor beside them. Shaun stood by the door, grim-faced, his arms folded. "I think we'd all like to know what's going on," he said pointedly.

Stella stared at the patterned rug on the floor. "I saw your puppies on your website, Shaun. One of them . . ." She nodded toward Koko, " . . . looked just like one of my own puppies."

"We know," Andi said, thinking of the impostor.

"So, I arranged to have them switched," Stella went on.

"Why?" Natalie burst out. "What's wrong with your puppy?"

"Nothing!" Stella looked shocked. "He's perfectly healthy! I just . . . Well . . . My stud dog passed away recently."

"I read on your website that Monty had died," Shaun said. "I'm sorry. That must have been a blow for you."

"It was more than a *blow*, Shaun. He was my *life*, and my source of income. I wanted to replace him with a better dog — a dachshund with cream genes — so I could breed puppies with cream coats. Like yours! Except there's no way I'd be able to afford one," Stella added bitterly.

"But your dogs do so well in shows," Shaun told her. "And they have good temperaments. Why do you care so much about the color?"

"*Did* so well, Shaun. My dogs haven't won in years. And you know cream dachshunds are more valuable." Stella stood up and began to pace. "When I saw on your website that a male puppy of yours, with cream genes, looked like one of mine, I knew I could switch them. I would never have shown your dog, of course, in case you recognized him. I would simply have used him to breed. In a generation or two, I could have produced a pure cream dog and the value of my litters would have soared."

"You should have come to me, Stella," Shaun explained. "I would have worked with you on a price."

"What, and have you telling everyone at the shows that my success is thanks to you? That I was your charity case?" she countered.

Shaun was clearly offended. "I wouldn't have — "

Stella didn't wait for an explanation. "You still have the same number of puppies, and more with cream genes!" she shouted.

Shaun paused for a moment, growing angrier. "I just

can't believe I'm hearing this! You stole *my* dog, just so *you* could make more money, and you're saying it's my fault?"

"To be honest, I'm impressed you even noticed it! I thought I gave you a perfect match," Stella noted, seemingly oblivious to the damage she'd done.

"For starters," Andi said, "your puppy doesn't have all Koko's cute little habits. And there's a keyhole-shaped patch on Koko's tummy that your puppy doesn't have."

"But what about *your* puppy?" Natalie asked Stella. "Don't you care about him?"

"Of course I do. I knew Shaun and Eleanor would make sure he went to a good home," she replied matter-of-factly.

"But how did you know when the puppies would be at the vet's for their shots?" Tristan asked.

"It was on the website," Andi said. "Eleanor told Zan he could check the site for the exact date."

Lance Sinden slumped back in his chair. "I can't believe this, Aunt Stella. You told me this was a practical joke, and that your *close friends* would think it was funny! I never would have gotten involved if I'd known the truth!"

Stella frowned. "It would have been worth it, if I'd gotten away with it. I could have become the country's leading breeder of miniature dachshunds."

Andi was shocked. She knew there were some ruthless dog breeders around — Zan Kirby had been investigating them, after all — but it was clear that money was the only thing that mattered to Stella Milton.

"I want you to come back to my house and get your puppy, Stella," said Shaun. "Then I want you to write to the Dachshund Breeders' Association and resign from the committee. You're going to tell them exactly what you've done."

Stella stared at him in horror. "I can't do that. I'll be banned from showing my dogs!"

"Good! You deserve it for what you've done to poor Koko and your own dog. Not to mention implicating your nephew in a crime he knew nothing about." Shaun was furious. "And, frankly, I think I'm letting you off easy by not reporting you to the police."

"I can't write to the committee. Dog shows are too important to me."

"It's up to you, Stella," Shaun declared sternly. "Either you write that letter or I go to the police."

Stella glowered at Shaun, but Andi knew it was only because there was nothing else she could do. There was no way she'd want the police involved.

"I'm so sorry about all this," Lance Sinden said as they left his apartment. "My aunt insisted it was just a joke." He shook his head and gave Stella an unhappy look.

"It's all right," Shaun said. "At least we've got Koko back now."

The Pet Finders piled into his car, and he drove them back to his house. Stella followed in her own car.

Andi held Koko on her lap. He'd fallen asleep with his head resting on her hand. Andi played thoughtfully with his whippy little tail.

Eleanor threw open the front door as they pulled into the Carters' driveway. "Is that Koko?" she cried as Andi climbed out.

"Yep!" Andi replied, beaming at her.

"Oh, thank goodness!"

Stella Milton pulled up on the road then.

Eleanor glanced at Shaun, clearly confused. "Stella Milton? What's *she* doing here?"

"Long story," Shaun warned.

In the living room, Tooey was pacing restlessly beside her basket. "It's all right, Tooey," Andi said, kneeling beside her. "Your missing baby's come home." She put the puppy carefully on the floor. Tooey gave a bark of recognition, then began to lick him frantically.

The other puppies bundled out and crowded around their brother, barking shrill greetings. The impostor puppy stayed in the basket, looking rather lonely. *He may not have the cream gene*, Andi thought, *but he's still adorable.*

Stella went over to the basket. "I guess Horace will be happiest back with his mother," she said, picking him up gently. "Hello, little guy." She smoothed his head with her hand.

Andi was relieved to see Stella had *some* feelings for the puppy, and he seemed content to snuggle down in her arms.

"His name's Horace?" Natalie asked.

"It's short for Midshipman Horatio. Not that it's any of your business!" Stella glared at Shaun and Eleanor. "Good-bye. I don't expect we'll be meeting again."

"I hope not," Shaun said, showing her to the door. "And don't forget about the letter, Stella. I expect to see a copy of it, so I know you've definitely sent it."

With that, Stella Milton stomped down the hallway and slammed the front door shut behind her. It was quiet for a moment once she'd gone.

"Isn't it great to see Koko back where he belongs?" Andi said as the little puppy followed Tooey to the basket, climbed in, and snuggled down beside her.

Before anyone could reply, Tristan's cell phone rang. "Oh, hi, Zan."

Andi and Natalie crowded around to listen.

"Good news," Zan said. "I've got the go-ahead for that article about the puppy switch. And the Pet Finders are going to be featured in a big way!"

"Excellent! But you're just in time to hear the *best* news — we found Koko!" Tristan said excitedly.

"Well done! Maybe we could get together for lunch at The Treetop Hotel so you can tell me all about it. I've heard they have great pastries."

"Sounds good," Tristan said, as Andi and Natalie giggled at the coincidence. "Can't wait!"

"I think you'll have to keep Stella's name out of the article," Shaun warned when Tristan had hung up. "Otherwise the police might get involved, and I promised her I'd keep them out of it."

"That could work!" Andi said. "Zan's article will be even more mysterious and exciting if he has to call the puppy thief *Mrs. X*!"

* * *

"How did you do?" Mrs. Talbot asked as soon as Andi opened the front door.

"Case closed! Koko's back with his mom and dad and brothers and sisters. And Horace, the switched puppy, has gone home, too."

Her mom gave her a hug. "Andi, that's great! Good job, Pet Finders!"

"Thanks!" Andi smiled. Finding Koko had been incredibly difficult — there'd been so many twists and turns, not to mention false clues that had led them in the completly wrong direction. But everything had turned out all right in the end.

"Okay, Bud," she said. "We have just enough time for some freestyling practice before dinner." The last part of her Talented Pets project was due at the end of the week. Her math and science work was complete, and so was her poem. She'd be asking her mom to help her make the video soon, so the more practice she and Buddy got the better. Hurrying into the living room with Buddy capering around her, Andi switched on the CD player.

As the music began to play, Buddy calmed down and came to stand in front of her. "Let's go!" Andi said, crooking her finger and beginning to walk forward.

Buddy backed away, keeping in time with her step.

After a few paces, Andi moved her hand to the right, giving the signal for a sidestep. As usual, Buddy moved his front feet first, then his back, instead of stepping with both at the same time.

"Come on, Bud!" Andi said. "Keep trying."

Even if he never got the hang of the step, it didn't matter. She'd always love Buddy, whether he was the best or the worst musical freestyler in the world. All his tiny little quirks were so memorable and loveable, she knew *he* could never be switched.

Thank goodness! Andi thought, and she kneeled down to hug him close.